Mississippi Prison Writing

MISSISSIPPI PRISON WRITING

ISBN-13: 978-0-9801944-6-3
ISBN-10: 0-9801944-6-6

Published by VOX PRESS 2021

Editor: Louis Bourgeois

Associate editors:
Becky Kelly
Nature Humphries
Simone Bourgeois
Margaret-Love Denman
Anne Steel
Marian Barksdale
Susan Marchant
Dianne Fergusson
Jeanne Hays
Shannon Lovejoy
Mari Kuhnle
David Shirley

Cover art: Betsy Chapman
Lay-out editor: Rayburn Publishing Design

Support for VOX's Prison Writes Initiative comes from the Mississippi Humanities Council, the COX Foundation, the Barksdale Reading Institute, the R&B Feder Charitable Foundation, the Maytag Foundation, the Dollar General Foundation, the Witter Bynner Foundation, the Resist Foundation, the Lamberth Foundation of Mississippi, the McCarthy Dressman Education Foundation, the Nora Roberts Foundation, the Gale Foundation, the Women's Foundation of Mississippi, the Puffin Foundation, A Blade of Grass Foundation, and the Ezra Jack Keats Foundation.

VOX and the Prison Writes Initiative would like to thank the Mississippi Department of Corrections for support of the program.

PRAISE FOR MISSISSIPPI PRISON WRITING

From the vivid details of the Vietnamese housing projects at the Bayou August Homes in East Biloxi, to the poignant descriptions of the quiet compassion among the elderly patients at the Parchman Disabilities Unit, the stories and poems of the Prison Writes Initiative provide glimpses into an "Invisible Mississippi" that are not traditionally associated with the narratives of Mississippi. What strikes me about the writers in the Prison Writes Program is how much of their writing gives a much-needed voice to the voiceless. These voices matter.

Don Allen Mitchell, *Delta State University*

Everyone's life is like a patchwork quilt with each of our life experiences sewn together to make us who we are. In this book we see through other's eyes tragedy and triumph, and anyone who reads it will feel sadness but will revel in the victories over circumstances that are told about here.

Keith Starrett, *United States District Judge*

While I was reading these stories, I reminisced on the adventurous memories made with my father before his incarceration 10 years ago. After reading Mississippi Prison Writing, I've grown more appreciative and empathetic, while also being inspired to continue advocating for criminal justice reform that includes keeping the bond between children and parents who are incarcerated. This is an important book and should be read by everybody.

Asya Branch, *Miss Mississippi, 2019*

Mississippi Prison Writing is an important read. The voices of those we've sent away from society "to do their time" should remind us of the common humanity we all share: the same hopes and dreams, the same fears and longings. Lend these writers your ear—they know what they're talking about from the inside.

p joshua laskey, *The Literary Review*

This collection of writing is raw and extremely important, as it gives a firsthand perspective from our fellow statesmen, women, and young people whom we forget, judge, and rarely hear from.

Ko A. Bragg, *Jackson Free Press*

Life is hard. You can't imagine how hard life is behind bars with no chance for parole. How does one DO THAT? How does one keep going in that situation? In *Mississippi Prison Writing*, the inmates are becoming writers….writing about their life. This is giving them a way to keep on keeping on with their day to day life. In any form, art is life giving and writing is a form of art that is bringing light into these prisoners' lives. These prisoners have time to think about life and living and their perspective is deep and important so read what they have to say about life here and you'll appreciate your own life more and you might learn something about living, too. I highly recommend this book.

Charlie Musselwhite, *Grammy award winning blues musician*

As a former resident of Mississippi and a journalist who has continued to report there, I know the sense of futility that can hang over that place—the feeling that all the opportunities of a modern, fair, "post-racial" America are far, far away. Things would seem to be especially futile in the state's prisons. Yet nowhere in this collection of writing by Mississippi's incarcerated men, women, and children does it overcome their deeper commitment to the expression of self. Some of these writers just keep a diary, marking each of their days with importance; others turn their analysis on the criminal justice system itself, because they know it best and want to contribute to the political conversation. Many essays recount the terrors of childhood in Mississippi, as if to say: this is what was done to my heart; it matters; let me tell you about it. One writer says, "Reality is I can die here." That may be true, but we can hear him clearly, thanks only to books like this.

Eli Hager, *The Marshall Project*

This newest release from Prison Writes Initiative is an intimate heart-talking encounter with dozens of men and women living in the extreme, stark conditions of Mississippi prisons. Each narrative, essay, journal entry, or poem appears in its raw, as-written state that lets each writer be real. This nitty-gritty work gets under your skin.

Lynne Elizabeth, *New Village Press*

A fascinating read from a multitude of voices inside prison walls. The stories run from the mundane to the intricate, including a real gem about the destruction of a Disney display by prison guards at Christmas. You don't have to condone or forgive what these people have done to just listen. You just might find they have a lot to say about life, death, and gaining a perspective on the time we all have left.

Ace Atkins, *The Sinners*

Among the broken hearts and broken hopes of this collection, one thing stands out—the importance of hearing these writers' special voices. The personal reflections of incarcerated authors describe predicaments and dilemmas that must be read to be understood. Perhaps with understanding … their own and our own … they can rebuild bridges to a kinder, gentler world.

Charles McNair, *Paste Magazine*

When you read the words in these prison journals, diaries and notebooks, it is a rare opportunity to peer through windows into the souls of real people, individuals, who each have a story and a different sum of life experiences.

Jay Hughes, *Mississippi House of Representatives*

The writers in *Mississippi Prison Writing* share their inner-most thoughts, opening their diaries for readers to witness actual daily life in prison, void of sensationalism and drama. The reflections offer frank meditations on regret, the monotony and isolation of incarceration, the often difficult and layered home lives before prison walls, the journey to self-realization. Though these writers are "reduced to living in a cage," their words leap off the page, gifting us with complex human beings fighting to keep spirit and creativity alive in a repressive system. They help us remember what happens on the other side of the wall, and why we should care.

Caits Meissner, *Prison and Justice Program*

Books are dangerous where there is injustice.

Jack Henry Abbot

Contents

Roger Ewing

Dead Man Walking

The subject for this paper has been on my mind for some time now. I hope I can give it the justice it deserves.

The subject is about life sentences and about the length of time one is supposed to serve. More importantly, what is the point of a life sentence? When does the correctional aspect change to punitive and retributive?

In the State of Mississippi prison system, life sentences fall into one of two categories: those sentenced before 1995 and those after. We will be writing about people sentenced after 1995.

A judge at the time of sentencing has the latitude to use discretion; he can impose a life sentence or life without the possibility of parole.

A life sentence in Mississippi is supposed to hold out the hope of eventual release to the one sentenced, but it doesn't. The Mississippi Prison System has in its lack of wisdom misinterpreted the law and holds the position that everyone has life without. We are not writing about the insanity of this position, but rather the effects it has on the individuals it is imposed upon.

In multiple studies done on the criminal justice system, it has been found that by taking the hope of eventual release away from a prisoner, you also take away the incentive to follow the rules, so to speak. You've created in essence an uncontrollable animal that answers only to itself for its actions. I am happy to report that not all prisoners stoop to this level of conduct.

I find myself in this situation with no hope of any type of future outside the prison system.

Like others, Ive gone through various stages during my incarceration.

First, I had to accept that I was even in prison and that I might not get to go home any time soon. I think you could say this is your bewildered stage. At the same time, you look at your surroundings and see they are simply terrible. The roofs leak, and the paint on the walls is drab and peeling off. Everything is filthy, and the toilets are overflowing. The food is bad and at times inedible.

You realize pretty quickly that the vast majority of officers you come into contact with all possess double digit I.Q.s, the inmates mostly at the same level. It took me about six months to accept my predicament and move on; some never do.

Then you enter a stage where you find ways to improve not only your living conditions but your legal position too. Most people do this and do it in various ways.

I decided to work and do the best job possible at any task I was assigned to. Need a really clean bathroom? I was the man for the job! This attitude upgraded me a year early from C custody to B custody, which entitled me to better housing.

I strived for years to show the Mississippi Prison System that underneath everything I was a model prisoner. I always worked, and I attended the Christian College. I took any available educational course to show I was a changed man. I volunteered at all the church services. I've taken care of Alzheimer's patients, I've always strived to be seen as part of the solution instead of part of the problem.

For what? Being someone completely different from the person I was all those years ago does not change a thing. The Mississippi Prison System says they will never release me under any circumstances.

So, the question still begs to be answered: when did the sentence cease to be correctional and strictly become retributive? Everyone is different, so their times will not be the same time as mine. Mine snuck up on me when I wasn't aware. What changed?

I woke up one day after spending 12 plus years just on Parchman grounds and asked myself, "What's the reason for my further existence?" There is none; with no hope for eventual freedom, what's the point?

So now I find myself as an elderly inmate in failing health with no viable reason for my existence. Again, what would be the point? When man does not have an obtainable objective to work towards, men tend to give up.

I've given up; I don't have a reason for my existence anymore. So what am I doing? I guess I'm sitting here waiting to die.

Forgotten: A Northern Jew in a Southern Prison

To be a Jew is a unique experience in itself. A Jew who finds himself in a Mississippi prison is in for an extraordinary experience, let me tell you.

Jews make up one half of one percent of the world's population. That is reflected in the prison population, also. I am incarcerated at the Mississippi State Prison at Parchman, Mississippi. For the first twelve years, I never heard of another Jewish convict; kind of amazing with a prison population that constantly hovers around 4,000 inmates. But Jews are a peculiar people; when we see trouble, we tend to disappear. It's an inbred trait, I believe. We've had a lot of accumulated experiences spread over the centuries.

While Jews live and work among the general population, we are a very distinguishable people. We have our own customs, traditions, and culture that set us, as a people, apart from everyone else. This makes us an easy target. Targeted by whom, you ask? The list is endless it seems at times. I'll try to write about a few to give you an idea.

Take for instance the prison guards. One must note that people that cook hamburgers at McDonald's make more money than an entry level guard. So, their IQ is in the double digits.

Because of work or religious-related issues, I find at times that it is necessary to inform the on-duty guard that I am Jewish. An easy task you would think, but I believe it would be easier to raise the Titanic. Most guards will look at you like you are a space alien and say, "What's Jewish?" You know your life just got more complicated. At times like that, I attempt to educate them on who and what a Jew is, which is hard for them to comprehend. Usually it boils down to me saying, "Jesus was a Jew." They all know who Jesus is, so they respond, "Jesus saved me; so what do you want?"

Mostly my problems are work-related. So, I tell them I need Saturday off because I will not work on the Sabbath. The typical response is, "Okay, you can have Sunday off." You try to explain that the Jewish Sabbath is Saturday but to no avail. You wonder if the person who hired them ever get arrested for premeditated stupidity.

You would think it would be easier to interact with the Chaplain's Department, which is composed of Christian Ministers. They go to school so they can become ministers, don't they? That's not a job requirement here at Parchman, evidently.

Every summer two Hassidic Rabbinical students from the Yeshiva University in NYC come to visit me. It is a requirement that they be accompanied by a chaplain while on prison grounds.

One year this chaplain brings the students to my housing unit. He decides he is going to sit in on the visit. This is against the rules. But no problem; we switched between a combination of Hebrew and Yiddish. The chaplain left the room in a huff because he couldn't understand a word.

After the visit was concluded and we were saying our farewells, the chaplain brazenly interrupted us and told the two students if they stopped wearing their grandfathers' clothes they would be taken more seriously. Only in Mississippi can an overabundance of ignorance be demonstrated in such a fashion.

Another time a Rabbi was kind enough to send me a Jewish study bible. The chaplain who brought it to me asked if he could look at it. After looking at it, he started looking at the box it came in. He finally looked at me and said very apologetically, "You got cheated; there's no New Testament!" It's hard for me to be humble around such mental giants.

Approximately fourteen years ago, the Baptist Theological Seminary started a program here at the prison. The stated objective was to train Inmate Religious Assistants, or I.R.A. The program would take four and one-half years to complete. At the end of that time, you would earn a bachelor's degree in Christian Ministry. Furthermore, you would be a fully qualified Southern Baptist Pastor.

The director of the school wanted to meet me. So, being both curious and polite, I agreed to meet with him. He turns out to be a big bear of a man with a domineering personality. It turns out I am really there so he could attempt to recruit me to be a student. The State mandated that people of other faiths be admitted to the program. It was an equal opportunity thing. I was there simply because I was the only Jew at the prison.

I had the director acknowledge I was a practicing Jew and, if I agreed to attend the school, I would most definitely still be one at the end. The school was an attractive alternative to the situation I was currently faced with. At least the school did not evolve animal manure, rakes, or shovels, and it was air conditioned. They got their token Jew; I got a life of comparative intellectual leisure.

For the next couple of years, I threw myself into this new endeavor with enthusiastic craziness. I preached Jesus and prayed for people to be healed. I did all the tasks laid before me exceptionally well. At the end of this wild ride, I became a Jewish Southern Baptist preacher. Who said God doesn't have a sense of humor? I am still a practicing Jew, and when my Rabbi comes to the prison to study the Torah with me, he calls me Padre. It was a grand adventure for a Jewish man to take.

As I stated earlier, Jews are targeted in prison and especially prisons in the Deep South. Why are we the target of so much hate and violence? Anti-Semitism certainly plays a big role with some groups. Men in their ignorance are afraid of what they don't understand. But I think the main reason is because we are few in number. People perceive weakness which equates to no retaliation, or so they think; so we are an easy target.

In today's prisons, prison gangs are the dominant force. One of the gangs is called the Aryan Brotherhood. The members are exclusively white male supremacists who have banded together for mutual protection. The way to gain entrance into the group is through acts of violence. They need a target. I'm handy.

Over the years, I've had multiple run-ins with this group, and it's never been good. In my early years here, I was forced to fight just to survive. I did not win one fight with this group over the years. If their first fighter was unable to produce the desired results, additional gang members would be added until I was overwhelmed. These shining examples of humanity are not the only gang that operates within the prison.

African Americans make up approximately seventy percent of the prison population in Mississippi. With such a talent base to draw from, they also have the largest gang membership. They literally dwarf the white gangs. Having the largest membership gives them control of the contraband trade, which is extremely lucrative. It consists of alcohol, tobacco, recreational drugs, cell phones, weapons, and anything else you desire. The quantities of contraband that move through the prison system on a weekly basis are truly staggering.

I vividly remember a package of fifty cell phones the authorities confiscated at one time. At three hundred dollars a phone, that is quite the bust. It is common for authorities to confiscate fifty pounds of tobacco at a time, or five pounds of marijuana. You would think that would interrupt the availability of these items, but you would be wrong.

How does this amount of contraband work its way into the prison system? The prison staff itself brings it in! When you pay your workforce the absolute minimum possible, expect corruption. These people need to support their families too.

Easy money has a way of being attractive. When guards can buy a pound of tobacco for twenty dollars at the store, legally, and then bring it into the prison system and sell it for two hundred dollars, what does anyone expect them to do? The state itself perpetrates the contraband trade and in turn fuels the senseless violence we are forced to live with.

I am what is known as a peon within the hierarchy of the prison. A person is considered a peon if he lacks an alliance with an established prison gang. I always thought it best not to owe any type of allegiance to such a group. If you do have an allegiance, you essentially become their puppet. They are then able to pull your strings anytime they choose, to make you do their bidding. The things they command you to do can be truly heinous or they would do it themselves.

I came to the realization that I had to protect myself. I had to come up with a way to make myself indispensable to all parties. This is not an easy task to accomplish as one might think. I needed to find the one thing everyone wanted in prison that I could provide. It also, by my choice, had to be completely legal.

After a strenuous search, I discovered the solution to my predicament. It had been staring me in the face all along. I became known within the prison as a Writ Writer. You would use the term jailhouse lawyer.

Everyone wants to get out of prison regardless of who they are. Most convicts and their families are unable to pay the high cost of a free world lawyer. Especially if their case is making its way through the seemingly endless appeal process.

I have two college degrees, and I'm Jewish. The greatest strength the Jewish people have possessed throughout history is our scholarly abilities. I allied myself with another writ writer and started writing his writs and court motions out for him. Over time, I got very proficient at it. So, it was time to hang out my shingle.

Every successful business develops a business plan. So that's what I did. My highest priority was to make myself so valuable to all parties that I would be under everyone's protection. To do this, I actively sought clients from the most powerful, prevailing gangs in the prison, and the strategy worked.

It soon became common knowledge that if you bothered me in any way you would have unwanted visitors. But I was careful not to alienate anyone because you never knew when you might need a friend.

I refrained from taking on cases that there was no prospect of making any headway on. I also did not take on every case that came my way. I always tried to keep in mind that I was not a trained lawyer. I felt that it would be despicable to deceive anyone about my abilities. Guess that fact would prevent me from becoming a real lawyer.

Now that I became an established and somewhat respected writ writer, life was easier. I was able to navigate prison society without having to constantly look over my shoulder. I had a little peace and security, finally. But my problems weren't over; they're never over in prison.

For my first years in the penitentiary, I was assigned to live in a dormitory-style building. It is common to find dormitories that were originally designed to house sixty men now housing one hundred and twenty men. Overcrowding is always an issue. At times I awoke in the morning only to discover someone sleeping under my bed.

Overcrowding breeds chaos, they go hand-in-hand. It is hard to assimilate the utter pandemonium unless you were to experience it firsthand. The level of noise which is always a dull roar never abates, not even in the middle of the night. The lights seldom go out. Card games are played around the clock, and you find men exercising at 3:00 a.m. The dormitory pulsates like a living organism ready to devour the unsuspecting.

The buildings themselves are in a state of constant disrepair. Toilets overflow because they won't flush, and windows will not close. Many of the roofs have deteriorated so badly that it rains inside the building just as much as it does outside. Water heaters that go out in the fall are not fixed until spring.

Introduce susceptible young men into the mixture and you have a disaster waiting to happen. These youngsters, out of sheer boredom, turn to drugs even though they understand the consequences of their actions. Young men are ruled by herd instinct; what one does they all do.

Drugs are like a rottenness sucking the life blood out of the prison population. Young men who are lured to the embrace of drugs act as if they are thoroughly ashamed of their very existence. They act as if they are possessed, and their dreams of their once innocent youth are forever shattered. The drugs have created monsters; I know because I live with the monsters.

Jews as a people live in the here-and-now. I was taught that concept since I was a small child. Witnessing to people becomes self-destructive, but I have a natural tendency to try to help these people. But that's against all prison rules.

When you enter prison, you are enjoining yourself to a culture foreign to the one you grew up in. Here in prison we have our own language and rules. The cardinal rule in prison is: "If it does not directly affect you, it's none of your business." It can be detrimental to your health to stick your nose in other people's business. In order for you to survive, you refrain from it. Doesn't mean when you see a suffering, struggling, or tortured human being, your heart doesn't go out to them.

When you first come to prison, you still have hope. You hope your family is all right. You hope that one day you might be able to return to them. The list would be endless, needless to say. Then you're introduced to the cauldron of chaos the prison administration expects you to live in; all hope ceases. When you take away all hope, when you treat people as if they are no better than animals undeserving of respect and compassion, do not be surprised one day when the whole group of them rises up and shakes off their bonds. This place is a powder keg just waiting to explode.

Have you ever thought about what the word hope means? The American Heritage Dictionary says it means: 1. To wish for something with expectation; 2. A desire accompanied by confident expectation. To wish for something: interesting, isn't it? There is an overabundance of wishing going on in here.

I have a more realistic definition that men in prison should utilize: hope is the lies we tell ourselves about the future. Don't expect anything, and you won't be disappointed.

For a Jew who tries to observe the laws of kosher, prison presents a challenging problem. What can you and what can't you eat? Prison food at best is substandard. Most times you probably do not know what you are eating and probably don't want to know. The food is stored improperly with rats getting into it. The cooks don't cook the food like it should be. Sanitation for the most part is nonexistent. Just this year alone, I have been hospitalized five times due to food poisoning.

I believe God looks at a person's heart to see if their intentions are righteous. I try to be very careful about what I choose to eat when I go to the mess hall. I miss a lot of meals because of it. I'm always hungry. Years ago when I entered prison, I weighed 190 pounds. Today I weigh 142 pounds, a big difference.

I have asked the prison administration for a kosher diet before, to no avail. To get a kosher diet in the state of Mississippi you would have to go to court. With so few Jews in the prison system, the chances of winning a court battle are slim. Without help from an attorney from the free world to guide you through the maze we call our legal system, it would be daunting. So I do without, but my fervent prayer is Ha-Shem will examine my heart.

There is a surprising amount of organized religion in prison. As troubled men, we seek solace, peace, forgiveness, and guidance. We have been humiliated, humbled, and stripped of our integrity and dignity. Many times, we have lost our friends, families, and assets. Most of us have absolutely nothing left; we have been cast into Sheol. So, in turn, our attention becomes focused upward.

The United States is supposed to be predominately a Christian country. If you are in prison and you're seeking the Christian God, in all actuality you are in a great place to accomplish that. We have four Christian chaplains working full time with the Chaplain Department. Then there are volunteer Christian chaplains. Also, there are numerous Christian organizations who come on a regular basis to minister to the men. The point being, the Christian faith is well represented here. Personally, I think that is great, and I envy them a little bit. At times, though, my heart seems to be wrenched out of my chest in pure agony as I watch them squander their chances to develop a meaningful relationship with the Christian volunteers.

These Christian volunteers donate their time to come here, sacrificing time with their own families to do so. These men are dedicated to their mission of changing lives; they come faithfully week after week. You can only admire these wonderful men.

The Muslims have an Imam on the Chaplain's staff. So now the Muslim inmates can come together and worship as a unified entity. The Muslims as a group are better organized than the Christians. If there is a problem that concerns them, they close ranks and speak with one voice. The administration has learned the hard way to treat these men with the respect they deserve.

If one takes the time as I have to listen and observe the Muslims, one can learn valuable life lessons. With them I have learned how to respect their religious views even though they differ from my own. I've had real life lessons on how to interact with men who have a different cultural background than mine. These two abilities are the key to getting along with any people, any group, anywhere in the world. In a sense, I find myself indebted to them. All in all, I've enjoyed a good relationship with the Muslims over the years while in prison.

The Jewish population is not so fortunate. If you noticed, I said Jewish population. A phenomenon has occurred! The Jewish population has actually doubled this past year, as of this writing. There are now two of us, unbelievable, but there are strong rumors that the other one had himself transferred to a better place. Ah, well.

As I stated, we Jews are not so fortunate. We don't have a rabbi on the staff of the Chaplain's Department; we don't have an advocate to represent us. Without an official voice speaking on our behalf, it's almost like we don't exist. It makes it easy to ignore us.

Unlike the Christians and Muslims, we are not overwhelmed with volunteers to minister to us. We have neither rabbis nor lay people who come to the prison. In all my years here only one rabbi came and was allowed to stay one hour; that was it. The two rabbinical students are allowed one-half hour every year, despite the fact they travel all the way from New York City. Mississippi is very generous with their time, inspiring others to make the trip. But what can one do? We have no one willing to speak for us.

As a result, you find out it is completely up to you to provide for all your spiritual needs. This is not an easy task to accomplish from within the prison. Especially if you have no assistance from anyone from the free world.

Take for instance the obtaining of addresses of area synagogues. It's an easy task for someone in the free world; just look in a phone book or on the internet. We in here are forbidden access to both venues. It took me five years to get the addresses, and then the first four I wrote did not respond. Gives a fella confidence.

But determination finally won the day. A rather large synagogue answered my letter and asked how they could assist me. I asked if it would be possible to provide me with a Torah or prayer book. They replied affirmatively and sent the items.

End of story? Most certainly not! Remember we were in Mississippi, home to the ignorant. Most Jewish ceremonial books are written in Hebrew on the right page and the left page has the English translation. Easy enough to understand, wouldn't you think? But when you contend with imbeciles of the first rank every day, nothing is ever easy.

So, I have to explain that Hebrew is the language of the Jewish people and that I am Jewish. Hence the Hebrew in the books. They think it is some kind of mysterious code. Then they would like to know what it says. Remember the English on the left page? Sometimes it is difficult to stay with them intellectually, but I make the sacrifice.

The books are approved and given to me only to be confiscated later by other guards. I now get books in the same vein sent in periodically. I use them for a while, then some Neanderthal comes along and takes them. I never have to worry about clutter or accumulating too many things.

While I have an endless amount of amusing stories I could tell about what the administration has done to me in the physical world, that's not what hinders me: it is the systematic mental torture I'm subjected to, intentional or not.

Have you ever been alone, truly alone? I'm not talking about going to the store alone or watching TV by yourself. I'm talking about being emotionally isolated from all human contact. How can this happen, you ask? It's through ignorance, unfounded hatred, prejudice, and anti-Semitism.

Even though I live in close contact with a hundred other men on a daily basis, I am for all practical purposes essentially alone. I've been alone for years, which puts me in a precarious position mentally because I am a Jew.

What have I done to combat this aloneness? I have done what Jews have done since time immemorial. I have turned my eyes towards my God. I have found I am alone no more; Ha-Shem is always with me, or so I believe.

As a youngster, I attended the obligatory Hebrew school held at the local synagogue until my Bar Mitzvah. As young men and women do the world over, I strayed away from Judaism, something I am not necessarily proud of, but such is life. When I came to the realization that I needed to turn to my God for my own sanity, I also realized I was inadequately prepared for the journey. Unlike the Christians, and to a lesser extent the Muslims, there is absolutely no support system in place for Jewish inmates in a Mississippi prison. It has been an uphill battle all the way.

It took me three years to secure my first Torah and TANAKH,

years later to obtain any prayer books. I have never been allowed anything else. I still have no rabbi I can turn to for instruction or advice. Over the years I've had to figure things out myself with Ha-Shem's help.

We Jews are a tenacious people, and as such, once we decide to do something, we never stop until the task is accomplished. This trait has served me well over the years, and I utilized it here too.

The Rabbis say that one of the highest forms of worship for a Jew is to study the Torah. I took that saying to heart and study a minimum of three hours a day, every day. I have discovered a lot of truths about Judaism in this manner. It is incredible what one can learn if one would set their head to it. When one studies alone like I do, one truly learns things for themselves. I know what I know because I discovered it myself. I can confidently take you into the TANAKH and show you why I believe what I believe. I have been "taught" very little about Judaism. But like Jews everywhere, at the end of a study session, I can come away with two opposing opinions.

This is not to say I wouldn't desire some rabbinical oversight, for I dearly would. I would even settle for another Jew to compare notes with occasionally. But through the years I've remained alone.

When I was a little boy, I grew up in my grandfather's household. One of my favorite memories is about my grandfather's relatives and friends from the old country that would come to visit and stay for a few days. The one thing they all had in common was the numbers they had tattooed on their left forearms. They had all been caught up in the Shoah and had spent time in the camps.

As a youngster I was allowed to listen as the grownups talked, as long as I was quiet. I vividly remember a man we called Bernie, who was asked one night what was the worst thing about his experience in the camps. He replied, "I felt I had been forgotten." That's all he said, but he said it with a measure of finality. I never forgot that night.

If someone asked me today what the worst thing was I had to contend with in prison, I would be compelled to say, "It is one thing to be lost and alone in a chaotic sea of humanity, but it is a true tragedy to be forgotten by your own people." I have been forgotten. An echo of Uncle Bernie's words from the past.

I looked in the mirror recently and saw an old man staring back at me; it kind of shocked me. Where have the years gone, I thought that day. Unfortunately, all this time I had believed in the fallacy that I was invincible. Turns out I wasn't.

Among the various maladies I now contend with is cancer, a respecter of no man. I have now had two strokes that have left me wheelchair bound. And as you can guess, my old ticker is not too good anymore. On top of all of it, as if that wasn't enough, I'm gradually going blind. But like Job, I don't blame my God. I have learned in life to take one day at a time. If one successfully completes this day, chances are good that tomorrow will take care of itself; it always does.

I am no longer in what is considered Main Population. Instead, the powers that be have decided to house me in a disability unit. For this I am grateful to the administration; it's almost like they have granted me a new life. Gone are the gangs and their senseless violence. I do not have to endure beatings anymore, and I've never had anyone sleep under the bed here.

It has all been replaced with full time nurses and officers who call you by your first name and genuinely care about your welfare. This unit I am currently housed in reminds visitors more of an old folks' home than a prison camp. Life has suddenly become a little more bearable. The worst thing I have to deal with now is some old geezer trying to hoodwink me out of my Jell-O; a bunch of tough hombres here.

Do I consider my life over? Most certainly not. I've got a few good years left in me yet. In the meantime, to keep my mind active, I take a college level Philosophy course. New ideas keep one's brain active and alert. I like to stay involved with life.

This is not all I do. A while back I was reading a religious-based article. It was explaining that God chose the Hebrew language to speak to the world through the Torah. The article went on to say God considered Hebrew to be a pure language and that it will be the language of heaven. Well, that sure caught this geezer's attention. So, yes, you guessed right. I am relearning Hebrew in my old age and doing quite well. Maybe I will have a need for it in the near future. With the rest of my time, I do as all old men do the world over; I sit and contemplate what's going to happen to me when I finally cross the river.

Discovering Yourself in Prison

If you ever have the unfortunate experience of finding yourself in prison one day, don't despair, for all is not lost. How can I qualify that statement? I'm in prison doing a life sentence and discovered who I really am.

Yes, it took me coming to prison to have the time to really examine who I was and how I related to society in general, but also to individual people. Sometimes, I discovered I did not like what I found within me. Prison gave me not only the time to really change within but also the opportunity. After all, prisoners have an overabundance of free time on their hands. It's up to them how they utilize it.

Most of the people you come into contact with in prison are dysfunctional and/or violence-prone and will remain so the rest of their lives. I made a conscious decision that I did not want to end up like that, and I make lasting changes where necessary. At times it's a painful and unpleasant endeavor.

A few years after I arrived at Parchman, I was given the chance to attend the New Orleans Baptist Theological Seminary's college-level program located at Unit 30. At first I was hesitant because being Jewish in a Christian program is a little strange. But I found out that a Muslim attended, and I took the plunge. I'm glad I did. I stayed there seven years, and it was time well spent.

Most of the men that attended were trying to change and live their lives right. If you're trying to change, it helps 'to be around like-minded people. I was fortunate in that aspect.

When one studies theology, one is pretty much forced into examining who they are, and this happened to me. The Bible gives many good examples on how to interact with others. The Christian Messiah, Jesus, is an excellent teacher in this area.

Take for example the Christian saying, "Treat others how you would like to be treated." Taken to heart and practiced on a daily basis, it is potentially life changing. Most folks don't want to be treated like garbage, so don't treat others like that. Easier said than done, it takes an attitude change. Again, it's not an easy job.

It takes compassion for others or a sympathetic feeling mixed with a little mercy to treat others fairly all the time. You have to dig down inside of yourself to find empathy for others; you have to work for it. Again, not an easy job.

After two strokes and a continuing battle with cancer, I am now housed in a Disability Unit. It's the perfect proving grounds to be able to demonstrate to yourself and others the changes in your persona.

For example, I am the main care giver to a 79-year-old Alzheimer's patient who on a good day just might remember his whole name. He has never spoken mine. I literally take care of all his needs. I wake him in the mornings, get him dressed, make his bed, make sure he goes to all the meals, get his laundry done and put up, and make sure he gets a bath regularly and gets his medicine, etc.

He also has a bad habit. He goes to the bathroom in his pants regularly. He wears diapers. When this occurs, no matter the time or what you yourself are doing, it's clean up time. Bath tub, here we come!

It takes patience, compassion, empathy, and a certain amount of love for your fellow man to continue doing this day in and day out. Otherwise your spirit would be broken and you would quit. I've done it for a year now. Do I get anything for it? No, not even a thank you. Will I continue? Yes, it's the right thing to do.

When I first came to prison, would I have been able to take care of someone in this condition? The answer would have to be no. I mentally would not have been able to handle it.

I'm ashamed of myself in a way, for it took me a trip to prison to change how I deal with others. Now I have a different outlook on life. So can anything good come out of a prison? Yes, it gave me a chance to reinvent myself.

Trauma

As this writer contemplated on what he was going to write about, he first did a word study on the word trauma and what its different variations meant. This is what he found:

trauma: a bodily or mental injury usually caused by an external agent; also a cause of trauma;

traumatize: to inflict trauma upon.

Word usage varies in different cultures and extends into different time periods. For example, the way a Pacific Islander utilizes a word could be very different from the way a European might understand it. The same would apply to a person from the 15th century versus someone from the 20th century.

This writer grew up in New York City during the 1950s and 60s, in a Jewish household. In that time period, children did not have traumatic experiences that changed one's life. Children had life experiences, and one moved on. In today's American culture, children move from traumatic experience to traumatic experience, seemingly without end.

In recent years here in the United States, there have been a rash of school shootings. A youthful gunman will enter a school, usually one they have attended, and shoot everyone in sight. Most times the gunman will continue upon his quest until either the police shoot him or he shoots himself, thereby ending a murderous rampage.

These actions precipitate the usual response. Grief counselors flood the scene to inform the survivors they have been through a "traumatic" experience and they're there to help them work through it. Let's not forget the shooter himself has been subjected to a "traumatic" childhood. Let's face it, that's why he shot his classmates to begin with.

The news media gets into the picture and reports on these "traumatic" events, thereby building on everyone's collective fears. Now the whole nation can experience these traumatic events themselves on the nightly news.

Let's look back to 1962 in New York City. This writer was just entering the 8th grade at a public school. The classroom he was assigned to was on the fourth floor with large windows overlooking the street. The teacher, a Mr. Rapport, enters the room after everyone is seated. He opens the window and dives out landing face-first on the concrete below. All the kids run to the windows to look at what happened to Mr. Rapport. Well, he most obviously was dead with a large amount of blood pooling under his body. Other teachers ran into the room to see what the commotion was about. After everything settled down, the kids were all sent home for a couple of days until the school could find a replacement for Mr. Rapport.

There were no grief counselors for us and no mention of the event in the news media. So much for "traumatic" events. After all, this was the 1960s in NYC where sh-t happens; you take it in stride.

This writer honestly does not remember having second thoughts about it, much less nightmares. The other kids did not seem overly concerned about it, and the event was quickly forgotten, except in the occasional crude joke on the playground.

Nevertheless, this writer continues his journey down memory lane looking for trauma. Here is another story he remembers.

When the writer was just seven years old, he was riding down the interstate at 55 mph with his family. His mother was driving and he was asleep in the front seat, leaning against the front door of the car.

Due to a mechanical failure, the door opens spilling the writer out on the pavement. The writer finds himself rolling down the highway at 55 mph like a bowling ball. Luckily he had fallen onto the emergency lane and was not hit by another motorist.

A state trooper had witnessed the whole event. He, along with my mother, decided a trip to the local hospital was prudent. The state trooper bundled the writer up in a blanket and placed him on the front seat of his cruiser. With lights and sirens going, the state trooper sped off to the hospital.

The doctors determined that, although the writer had a broken arm and lots of scrapes and bruises, he would live. It was decided the writer would remain in the hospital for two days, where he was the center of all the nurses' attention. Cookies, candy, kisses, and hugs were lavished upon him in abundance.

Upon his release from the hospital, this treatment was continued at his home by family and neighbors.

On returning to school, the writer found he was now a celebrity, if not a downright hero. Everyone wanted to sign his cast and touch the various bandages he was wearing.

Looking back, the writer does realize he had experienced bodily trauma, but he did not really experience mental trauma from the incident.

The writer got to ride in a police car with the lights and siren going, a pretty big deal to a young boy back then. He was the Center of Attention, both at home and in the hospital, something out-of-the ordinary in a large family. He was a celebrity at school for a time; there was nothing wrong with the situation. Was he traumatized? Only when it all ended!

In retrospect, we find that word usage is relative to both the culture in which the word is used and the time period when it is used.

Did children have traumas when this writer was growing up? The answer is no; we had Life Experiences. We learned at an early age to "suck it up." Crybabies were kicked to the curb.

This writer does have sympathy for the professor of this class, for he will surely be traumatized by this writer's writing before the end of the semester!

The memories whip through my mind like the winds of a storm through the treetops, and like lightening, the images flash in my eyes. But I can't grasp them anymore. They're like tendrils of smoke—dense enough to get you a bit choked up but not dense enough to do any harm. The noxious elements are now torpid. The flames are gone. I would never have thought I would say this, but I miss the sting, the burn of it. Now that there is no scream, I long to feel—just feel—anything. It's so hollow inside me now.

Oh, I remember, how well I remember waking with a start: my confused, frightened heart pounding in my chest, in my head. Too cool were the sheets clinging to my sweat dampened body, the violent shaking. My fists clenched so tightly that the crescents left behind by my nails will leave bruises again, perhaps above, perhaps below, perhaps over the indentions that already sleep blue and green in my palm. The terror I felt each time I woke to the sound of that relentless scream; the pain, the anguish in it chilled my bones. I could feel the tortured suffering resonate from the octaves of her voice. Then sitting there alone in the darkness, I would realize, yet again, why no one came running to her aid, not even to investigate the source of these blood-stilling ejaculations of agony. It wasn't because no one cared but because no one knew. I alone could hear her. I alone was aware of her deafening screams. I alone could hear her dying . . . But why? Well, because she was in my head—it was me all along—dying.

As long as life remains, I will never forget the moment she died. I felt it for she was wrapped deeply in the layers of my being. One moment the screams had, as usual, sent me dancing along the perilous edge of sanity with their endless peals of misery. The next moment, it stopped, simply and abruptly, ceased to be. As if it had never been. One would think I would feel relief, peace, even joy, but I felt nothing. Absolutely nothing. She was dead; I felt her die. The last scream cut short, then she was gone, simply gone into nothingness; taking with her my ability to feel, my essence and humanity. There was no sense of her fading, slowly seeping away. I was just completely alone, and I felt nothing.

They say that which does not kill you makes you stronger, and there's also some senseless bullshit about God not giving you more than you can bear. Well, what if it does kill you but your body doesn't die? What if the shell remains whole and intact but all that lingers are the shadows, the memories of a life lived, an existence cut short, and the sticky scorched muck left behind when pain and despair have seared a living, vibrant soul from its earthly body? The only residue in the shell is Pain and Shadows. That is all that I am. Raw and bare to the world. Naked, alone, and shivering. In my quest to feel, to find any emotion that would assure me that I am alive, I found rage—only rage. All I have to protect this thing that I am, this un-whole being from the abyss of utter nothingness is rage. Sheer, blood-boiling, animal fury. Rage at his killer; rage at the church that turned their backs on our orphaned children; rage at the community that attacked them; rage at the people who claimed to be family and friends then lined up to fabricate so they could play victim in the eyes of society who chose to be chattel, too lazy, too high, or too stupid to think for themselves; rage at a justice system which is neither kind nor just; rage at a correctional facility that not only refuses to facilitate correction but effectively and efficiently transforms its captives into the monsters society wants to believe we are.

This, this is what they made: no apology, no remorse, abandoned to this—this monster they have made of me. Me, all that is left of a beautiful person in a beautiful life. Now only an empty beast searching for an end to its misery.

And now this man asks for my emotions. My dear sir, you know not of that which you ask. I am a passionate being with only one emotion that drives me forth. And pages are to contain me?

I think not.

Charged Up

I slowly wake up because something disturbs my sleep. As I open my eyes, I find myself lying in an institutional, gray, 8x4 prison cell. A roving searchlight momentarily floods the cell with light from a window high up on the exterior wall. It gives me an uneasy surreal feeling. I run my hand through my hair only to find that my head has been shaved bald.

I become aware of multiple booted feet marching in unison coming towards me from a great distance. I turn and look through the metal bars that comprise the front wall of the cell. It is abnormally dark, but I can see two lines of large men dressed in military style clothing approaching the cell where I lie.

They stop in front of the cell, and I hear a key being inserted in the lock. It has an ominous sound. A large man fills the door opening. A deep voice booms throughout the cell, announcing, "It is time." There was a note of finality in his voice.

I am placed between the two rows of men, and we march away. In the distance, I can make out a doorway with bright white light pouring out. As we get closer, I can make out a large wooden chair bolted to the floor. The two lines of men stop before it. I see a large cable snaking across the floor, attaching itself to one of the legs.

Strong hands grab my arms, and I am forcefully seated in the chair. As leather straps bind me to the chair, my nostrils fill with the distinct odor of furniture polish; the wood is smooth beneath my fingers. Cold water runs down my back as a sponge is put on the top of my head. Next, a metal helmet with wire secured to it is strapped to my head. I can hear the men retreating. A voice asks if I have anything to say. I don't respond; I am all alone.

I feel as if I'm having an out of body experience. I'm floating above my body, looking down upon the room. I see a man with his hand resting on a large metal switch. Another man is having an earnest conversation on a telephone. He hangs the phone up. I notice a clock above him that reads 11:59.

The man with the phone has a somber look on his face as he turns and nods at the other man. Fingers wrap around the heavy switch. I can see the muscles of his forearms strain as he pulls the switch down completing the circuit.

I feel electricity coursing throughout my body. It raises me off the seat making me strain against the leather straps. My insides boil as if there's a volcano spewing molten hot lava within me. A scream dies on my lips as flames shoot out of my eye sockets and I see no—

More . . .

In my opinion, it was the switch that controlled the electricity that was connected by big cables to the electric chair. The base of the switch was made of a dark wood overlaid with a thick rubber pad. The switch itself was made of a dull, heavy looking metal. The end of the handle was also covered with thick rubber. The whole apparatus had an evil sinister look about it.

The hand that hovered over the switch was large and covered with coarse dark hair. The fingers were fat, and the nails were well manicured. There was a sheen of sweat covering the hand that glistened in the light. The hand had a noticeable tremble the entire time.

The main focus of attention was riveted upon the switch. You knew this was the instrument that was to deliver the coup de grace once the switch was thrown, with the electricity flowing through out your entire body. You began your dance with death, and you started on the journey into the Abyss.

The Room

The room in which I live measures 22 feet by 21 feet. The floor is comprised of 462 off-white floor tiles, each measuring 12 inches. by 12 inches. The interior hallway wall is 21 feet long and 10 feet high. It has a green, heavy steel door in the center measuring 8 feet high and 3-½ ft. wide. It has a wire mesh viewing window in it. The wall is finished with plaster. The two side walls are made of cinder blocks, each measuring 15 inches by 8 inches, each wall contains 240 of them. There is a 4-foot. florescent light fixture 8 feet off the floor in the center of each wall. The back or outside wall is also 21 feet long by 10 feet. high. There are two windows in it measuring 3 feet by 6 feet. Each window has 25 glass panes. The ceiling has two rows of three florescent lights, each light being 4 feet long. There are six metal beds, three on each side of the room bolted to the floor. Each bed is 2-½ feet wide by 6 feet long, all of them painted black. By each bed is a stand-up white locker 4 feet high. You get a warm fuzzy feeling every time you enter this cheerful, love-infested room.

Note: This story contains 199 words and is the best this shackled writer could manage.

Carla Hughes

Prison Journal

1. Today has been a tough day for me. The thing is, I really don't know why. There is no specific incident that's bothering me. I guess it's just a collection of everything. What we call "One of those days." Here, in prison, when someone says that, everyone instantly understands the weight of the statement. We understand that, at that point, everything is so overwhelming that you can't even put it into words. That's the day I'm having.

On the flip side, I really enjoyed my writing class today. We had a visiting professor who spoke on art and literature, and what characteristics makes them "good." I had never really thought of that before. So now, I'm going through my mental catalogue of books and rating them on their level of "goodness," what things make them that way and why certain books didn't make the cut. I like this exercise. I think that opening my thought process up in this way will significantly help my writing skills. I'm excited about this class, and I'm very thankful that our administration is open to us having this type of opportunity. You know what? Just reflecting on this one blessing, in comparison to the lack of opportunities for Joseph Dole (our reading assignment author) within his prison environment, has helped to make my day a little better. We sometimes focus on everything that's wrong and what we don't have, instead of looking at what we do.

2. I want to write a book. I always have! For as long as I can remember, I've always enjoyed making up stories, plays, commercials, songs, etc. I just enjoy writing. I can vividly remember receiving my first computer for Christmas when I was a young girl. My dad built me a desk with all these shelves and drawers. He and my mom filled them with books of poetry, novels, and all sorts of writing utensils. So, of course, this instantly became my "office" for writing and creating. I

can't even count the number of stories, plays, newspapers, magazines, etc. that I created in that space. Thinking of it now, I regret not keeping those writings. I would love to reread them now and revisit my teenage thoughts and creativity. Once I became an adult and started teaching, I used my love for writing in all my classes, regardless of the subject. I also wrote many of our school skits and programs, as well as grants and proposals for our school to receive funding for various programs. Now that I am incarcerated, I still use my writing skills. I continue to write creative stories in an attempt to escape my reality. I also use these skills to write and to help others write, legal documents and institutional requests of grievances. Writing is vital in the progression of every field, career, and aspect of life, professionally or personally. It has been a large part of my life, and I look forward to taking it even further.

3. Yesterday I mentioned wanting to write a book. I wasn't specific in that statement. What I actually meant is that I want to be a published author, because in actuality I've written many books. In just the time of my incarceration, I've written at least five novels. However, I am clueless on publishing procedures. I once ordered a book that was supposed to tell me everything I need to know about publishing. Well, it told me so much that I closed the book more confused than when I started. Another source of confusion for me is deciding what genre of writing I want to do. One of my books was a motivational guide for teen and young adult girls. Another one was what we call "Black Author," which I think is actually labeled as "Urban" writing in the bookstores. Then, I also started writing an autobiography about my life and this experience, as well as a few children's books. So, I'm kind of all over the place. I know which types of writing are easier for me, but I don't necessarily want easy. Another daunting task with writing while incarcerated is doing everything manually. It would be so much more helpful if we had a computer lab. It's something we should have anyway to help with our legal documents and other personal files. Now that I'm mentioning it, I wonder why we don't have a computer lab or physical library here. That's something I want to seriously look into!

4. Today I am disturbed by something my son told me. I called home, and my son, Landon, expressed to me that he and my mom

had to meet with the principal of his school. This took me by surprise because my son has never had any disciplinary issues in all his years of schooling. I quickly inquired about the nature of the meeting. My son went on to explain that he's being bullied by three boys at school. Honestly, my initial reaction was to laugh at this statement, because surely it's another one of Landon's jokes. I mean, physically, my son is one of the largest kids in his grade, by height and weight. He is also one of the few Black kids in a predominately white private school. On top of those things, he's an athlete with what I've always known to be a very confident and self-aware personality. Surely, someone like that doesn't get bullied, right?! Well, stereotypically that's what we think. We think that only kids who are considered different, weird, or outcast qualify to be bullied. Not true! My son is being bullied, and so much so that my parents had to enlist the help of the administration. This bothers me! Especially with the rise of teen suicides due to bullying. So I'm angry, but I try, however, to put my anger aside and just listen to my son's thoughts and feelings about the situation. I say a quick prayer in my mind before responding because I want to give him the best advice possible. But what is that? On one hand, you want to tell your child to do as the Bible says, turn the other cheek and pray for those who offend him. But, on the other hand, you want to tell him to stand up for himself and fight back if someone physically hurts him. Well, I did my best to find a middle ground and lead him in the right direction. By the time we ended our calls, he seemed to be in better spirits. So, from this point, all I can do is pray for God to help my son through this situation, without it breaking his spirit and self-esteem, as well as ultimately using this obstacle as a means to build his character.

5. Today was a good day! For the first time in a very long time, we were allowed to have a Field Day. That's when all the female inmates are allowed on the yard together. Which is not a small feat! By my calculations, that's easily over 500 women inmates in one place, at once, without extensive security. It clearly shows the administration's trust in us and their willingness to give us opportunities to have events. I am very thankful for that because it is not something they have to do. I am also very proud of all the women today. There was not a

single incident or altercation. Everyone enjoyed the chance to socialize with friends we don't always get to see; as well as to partake in the refreshments that were offered to us: hot dogs, popcorn, and juice. In the three hours we were given, some people chose to sit and enjoy the nice, cool day. While others, like me, played a variety of sports like volleyball, basketball, and softball. Overall, everyone who came out today enjoyed themselves. Hopefully, this will open the door for future programs and events.

6. Today is Super Bowl Sunday! I'm excited, not only because I'm an avid sports fan, but also because of the collective excitement of the zone. Everyone has pitched in to throw a Super Bowl party, even those who don't normally follow football. There is just an air of togetherness, fun, and friendship running through the zone, and that's not always the case. Whenever we can be in one accord with something, it's really refreshing!

7. We didn't have class today. It was kind of a bummer because I was looking forward to it. It's nice to get out of here at times. Plus, I just enjoy class. I love learning! I always have. When I was younger, I would always be teased and called a nerd. It never bothered me, though. Actually, I liked it. My family is big on education (both my parents are teachers, so I guess that's fitting); nothing less was accepted. But beyond that, I just enjoy learning new things. It excites me. One of my favorite things to watch is the MPB channel, where they play all the documentary shows, history shows, and nature shows. It always amazes me to learn about the things of this world and how everything fits together. Anyway, with that said, I'm really eager for us to get deep into this class and begin learning some new things.

8. I won't lie. I'm not looking forward to writing in this journal for another two weeks. It feels like a chore to me right now. Mainly because my days are redundant. I feel like my thoughts are, too. Because my schedule is so routine, I don't feel like I'm contributing anything fresh or new. I guess I'm just rambling, and who would want to read that? No one! I don't even want to write it! Hopefully tomorrow will be more eventful, and I'll have more to say. But today was bland. I woke up, took a shower after lunch (after waiting over an hour because we only have three showers for 145 women), fixed something to eat

out of my locker, watched a few reality shows on TV, and wrote this paragraph, and now I'll probably go back to sleep. I feel disappointed that I didn't do more. Tomorrow will be better.

John Barnett

Good Things about Prison

To be honest, prison has its good points, even if we don't want to admit it. We are always looking at one thing: we are locked up; we have lost our freedom; when are we getting out?

Once we stop blaming others and take responsibility for our actions, then we will begin to feel free inside. Let's face it, no one put us here but ourselves. We thought we could get away with what we were doing, trying to be clever, but we got caught. I believe in second chances, and no matter what you've done, you have to make things better. First, it starts with a positive attitude, especially with the Parole Board. They want to know your background, what you've done, if you've taken any courses that would change your life. You are going to hear many negative things in prison: there's lots of pessimistic people in prison who want to keep you down. I try to stay away from people like that, and I believe if you use the tools that prison has to offer, you will do better. I went back to school and got my G.E.D. I am in my sixties: prison helped me to get my G.E.D. When I get out, I want to attend a Junior College. I have met people here in prison who have bachelor and master degrees they got while in prison. Some of our famous people have been in prison.

Where I Got My Education

As we were about to start class, the teacher gave us some papers to read. The teacher caught me off guard because we were to go over one of the student's papers from the week before. As he was handing out the papers, he told us what the papers were about: Malcolm X. I thought to myself, why would I want to read about Malcolm X? First of all, we had nothing in common. He was Muslim, and I'm Christian. Our beliefs are different. There was another catch. The teacher had each one of us to read a few sentences. Man was I surprised! I was not expecting to hear what was being read about Malcolm X and how he received his education. As I read, I could relate to him. Prison was where I started to study, just like Malcolm X. I started reading and studying in prison. I can remember that I couldn't spell; it was awful! Most times, it would take me a week or better to write one letter. I could read pretty good, but that was about it. In 2009, I enrolled in a G.E.D. class in George County. I was the oldest guy in class. I studied and studied in 2010. The chaplain came to me where I was working in the prison kitchen. The chaplain said, "I need to talk to you." As we were walking to another room, thousands of things were going through my mind, mostly about my loved ones: were they okay? Most times, when the chaplain comes and ask to talk with you, it's not good news. But this time it was different, and with a big smile he said, "Mr. Barnett, you have passed the G.E.D. test." As I thanked God, I thought about how long it had been since I was in school. There are not a lot of things I have accomplished in my life. My G.E.D., I am proud of it. Might not mean anything to anyone else, but it means the world to me. I'm not ashamed of my spelling now. I can write much better and much faster today. I do believe the mind is a terrible thing to waste. When I talk to other inmates, older or younger, I try to give them confidence by allowing them to know that if I can do it, they can, too. In this day and age, you cannot get a job without a high school diploma or a G.E.D. I have talked to guys who have been in prison ten, twenty, thirty years. They don't believe they need an education. They are still in denial.

My Room

Welcome to my room here at Parchman, Unit-31. It's a lot smaller room than I am use to being in, but it's a lot bigger than the other rooms here at Unit 31. This room is the Support Room. The Support Room has its benefits; we have a big TV. Here, some of us even have our own TV. When you move into the Support Room, you're required to help out as needed. When you're in the Support Room, there's a good chance you won't be discharged as long as you behave yourself. There are other benefits: you can use the exercise machine when they call yard call.

Other inmates don't have this opportunity. This is a hospital, and you are here to recover. Plus, our rooms are clean and quiet. It has three big windows: lots of sunshine comes in the room, and it is quiet in the day time. If you want to study, you can. No one will bother you. Most of the time, the inmates stay to themselves. There's lots of electrical outlets in this room. This room has a nice view if you like looking at animals as they forage for food, or counting the cars and trucks as they pass down the highway. This room gives you the best view. Most of the inmates in this room have positive attitudes. They are looking forward to getting out one day.

My Dreams

The dreams I dream are serious to the point I am afraid to go to sleep. I pray no one else has these types of dreams. I don't know why I have these dreams. Am I being punished for all the wrong I have done? I don't want to go to sleep. I know the demons are coming. The dreams take me places I've never been, roads I never traveled, cities I never saw. Here I am, looking for that person who I want to kill: please let me wake up! I've found the person I am looking for. I wonder does he know why I am here? Is he dreaming,? Is he puzzled as hell like me just before I pull the trigger? I awaken. I have to use the restroom. As I walk down the hall, I pause; I pinch myself, to be sure I am not still dreaming. No one is up. The guards are sleeping at their station. What would they do if they knew the dreams I was having? Would they lock the unit down? As I get back to my room, I check the time. It's one o'clock in the morning. There's nothing to do. My bed is there. My eyes are heavy. I try to fight the sleep. I hate turning into this person. It's like doctor Jekyll and Mr. Hyde. How do I fight this demon? I got to go to sleep! Will I drift off to wake up to have my Miranda Rights read to me? Scientists have put men on the moon, seen galaxies trillions of miles away. Why can't they explain my dream? Am I going to take my dream to my grave not knowing?

Written in the Night at Parchman Farm

I've been locked up for such a long time: they took my freedom; now they want my mind. It's hard to stay focused in a place like this, surrounded by steel bars and barbed-wire fence. This is prison; my whole world has changed. They call me by number and not by name. They escort me everywhere I go; they shake me down from head to toe. This is their world; you have nothing to say. All of my rights have been taken away. They let you know so you won't forget that you are a convict. They've tried hard to break my will; they take our clocks and watches so that time will stand still. Yes, it would be nice, yes, nice for us all, if we could look up and see a clock on the wall.

JENNIFER DILLON

Prison Notebook

Feb. 1st

Today I woke up in a good mood. I always try to keep a smile on my face no matter the circumstances. As long as I steer clear of the drama, I can be as happy and stress free as I want to be. The best time of my whole day in here is talking to my son on the phone at night; because of that, I am able to sleep well.

Feb. 2nd

I'm aggravated at the way the guards talk to us in here. It's like they forget we are humans too. The only difference between them and us is that they didn't get caught. By the way some of them act, I know they don't walk a straight line out there in the free world. I feel like if they would treat us with a little more respect, they would most likely receive the same.

Feb. 3rd

I really appreciate the fact that we get the privilege to attend classes like this writing class. I love to write. When I was in grade school, I used to sit in my room and write poems. I find that writing actually relaxes me and takes me out of the reality that I'm in at that particular time. I've even considered writing a book one day.

Feb. 4th

I feel bad for the elderly women that have to live here. There is so much chaos that goes on from time to time, and they get affected by it. Like this big move, for instance; the older women had a very hard time getting all their stuff way over here. They should have kept all the woman age 50 and older in the 2A building. I understand that no matter the crime, you have to do the time, but at least do the time in better conditions.

Feb. 5th

I will never forget my journey when this is all said and done. I have really learned some lessons on this trip. I also learned a lot more about myself than I knew before. All I know is that when I do get released, I am going to be a different woman than the girl I once was. I've come a long way since last year, and I still have a longer way to go, but I'm confident about it.

Feb. 6th

Today was a good day. I received some good news. My sister, who is also my best friend, got married to her longtime boyfriend, and now she's pregnant! I'm just so happy how everything in her life is coming together. I'm so proud of her and the woman she has become. I can't wait until I get to a point in my life when she can say the same about me.

Feb. 7th

This zone can get very challenging to live in. I have to remind myself to watch who I befriend. I've learned time and time again in life that everybody is not your friend. As much as I would love to know that we all love and care for one another, there is still evil in the world. People confide in you, and as soon as you let your guard down, that's when they turn on you and reveal their true colors. Never trust nobody as far as you can throw them.

Feb. 8th

I enjoy the outdoors and sports. When I was in middle school, I was in just about every sport there was at my school. Track was my favorite. I really would enjoy if we had more sport activities in this compound. I think it would keep a lot of the violence down. People just like to have a good time by letting loose and having fun.

Feb. 9th

Time feels like it's slowing down. I try to get involved with the different programs, such as church, gym, movie day, etc. Sitting around the zone all day just makes time feel like it's at a standstill. Some days are just going to feel this way. Then there's the days where the whole day flew by.

Feb. 10th
Last night I had a dream that everybody was leaving to go home. I'm hoping that means that I will be leaving soon. I am ready for the day to come. I try not to think about it so much because it will slow it down. Sometimes you just can't help the feeling, though.

Feb. 11th
The phrase "love is blind" is so true to me. You have to be careful who you fall in love with. Sometimes you can't help who it is, but then that person winds up hurting you to the point to where you regret ever even speaking to them, much less falling for them. That's exactly why love is blind.

Feb. 12th
I'm learning to stop being afraid of doing something I want to do, but worried about the outcome. Life is about taking risks. You have to make mistakes in order to learn from them. I shouldn't care what people think about the choices I make in my life. It's my life, and I'm going to live it the way I want to live it.

Feb. 13th
I am a nice person, but some people take my kindness for weakness. I don't like to run around with a constant attitude just so people will know not to play with me. That's how I think you have to be with certain people, though, because they don't know any other way but violence. I grew up in a rough neighborhood and had a rough life, but I didn't let it affect my attitude toward other people.

Feb. 14th
Today is Valentine's Day! A day to show your significant other how much you love them. I really enjoy making cakes and surprising my lover by wearing sexy lingerie and heels. I can't wait to be able to do things like that again.

Feb. 15th

One day I would love to get married. I feel like every woman should get married once in their lifetime. I just know when I get married I am going to have the best wedding I've ever seen. I've always dreamed of having a big wedding with somebody I knew in my heart I wanted to spend the rest of my life with.

Feb. 16th

I have to break this cycle of prison. I never want my son to end up in such a horrible place like this. I know that I have to make some serious changes in my behavior, because what he sees his mom do, he will want to do. I know this because I did the same thing by following my mother's footsteps.

Feb. 17th

I am to cut my hair today. I was worried that I wouldn't like the length. I am learning to just take chances and face risks. I will never be able to do anything worth doing if I'm afraid of the outcome. I've decided not to play it safe with my life anymore.

Feb. 18th

Today was a very slow and gloomy day for me. I need to sign up for some activities to help the time go by. Right now just sleeping the day away is not going to cut it. I'm a very active person at home in the free world. It's easy to get into the routine of doing nothing if that's all you have to do.

Feb. 19th

I appreciate everything my family does for me in here. Sometimes it seems like I take them for granted, but not intentionally. When I realize how I'm acting towards them, I check myself, quickly. I don't know what I would do in here without my family's help. I believe that hard time in here is when you don't have anybody on the outside helping you.

Feb. 20th

I really am enjoying this writing class. Being able to express myself on paper however I want to is good for me. It gives me time to think about what I want to say and different words I would like to use to explain it. It keeps my brain running daily. Filtering through my experiences, I find out things about myself and the world I didn't even know. Writing is becoming one of the better parts about my life inside of prison.

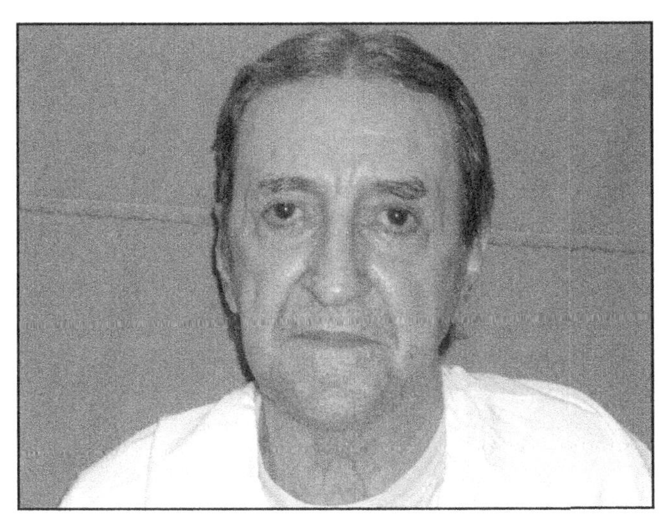

Larry Hurt

PRISON JOURNAL

Being that Prison Life is pretty superfluous, I find that it is better for me to write my thoughts down on a weekly basis. The repetition of logging in the everyday events seems to be a waste of words. Prison life is a boring existence. That is how the system is set-up. Change causes emotional distress in a prisoner that the System tries to avoid. Pacified prisoners are good prisoners.

Week #51 – 2017: This week we had our final class for the year. There was a small party and a program of the prisoners' reading their weekly assignment. We had a chance to interact with the producers of the program. I believe it all went very well.

Being this close towards the end of the year usually has a tendency to cause oneself to look back over the past year and reflect on the position you find yourself in and what brought you to where you are today. Easier to look at a year than to look over your past life. Christmas is just around the corner, then the New Year. 'OH Boy,' start all over again.

Week #52 – 2017: Christmas is over and now it's time to start an evaluation on life overall.

Some unsettling news from the only outside contact I maintained this week. It seems that a close relative has made an effort to make contact with me after 35 years of silence. A lot of mixed emotions about this. Brings back some good but mostly bad memories. It's not that I don't love this individual; I do with all my heart. It will be interesting in seeing how things play out, but at the same time, I like the distance that time has created: protecting my emotions, I suppose.

Week #1– 2018: The problem with getting old is that, while you are young, you don't have time to dwell on what you are doing or have recently done. It keeps a conscience clear and doesn't impair your judgment at a time of crucial decision making that can alter your destiny.

Then finally what you strive for in your everyday fight to continue towards the ultimate goal, the last man standing, you reach that or near to it, and realize that it's not all that it's cracked up to be. You're alone in your thoughts, in a body that will not perform death-defying feats any more or any other feats without the aid of pharmaceuticals, if you get my drift.

Week #2 – 2018: Not much excitement, except for a mentally challenged individual dying—can't say an inbred retard anymore—and making the local and national news.

Pretty dull week. Just reflecting on the past sixty plus years of survival and noting the mistakes that can't be repaired and questioning your own judgment.

Still reading during the working hours to avoid the reality of where you are and the series of events that has led up to this precarious situation.

Week #3 – 2018: It has been even a slower week. Just feeding the critters as, Ellie Mae Clampett would say. At least they are somewhat free. They are still prisoners of nature, though. No matter where you are or what you are, if you live and breathe, then you are a prisoner.

There are many kinds of prisoners. We here at Parchman are just one of many kinds. Being a prisoner here has some sort of freedom. The longer you do time and stay out of trouble, then the more freedom you are allowed.

In the free world, people are prisoners of their environment. We tend to chain ourselves to a typical way of life. You need food, water, and shelter. You are born into prison of the environment that surrounds you. So is every living thing.

When I hear people whine about being locked up in prison, I tell them that they need to look on the bright side. "They can't eat you—legally." I have been to where you had your doubts about what you just ate.

*week 6: This week we had another fellow inmate leave us. Although it was feet first, which was probably the only way he was going to escape us here at Clinic #31. He was up in his years and was ready to go.

Looking back at the year I've spent here at 31 and around 42, seeing the ones go feet first has an impact on everyone. It's surprising how the death of an inmate, even the ones we barely know, affects us all. But we also have just a hint of a smirk on our faces knowing that the system can't punish them anymore.

Unfortunately this is how most of us will go out. Sometimes I thank God that the medical treatment we get is of the lowest quality. That just means we will beat the system faster than the judge was thinking when he passed sentence on us. But the sad part is that an empty bed available means that some poor fool will fill the void as quickly as possible, and so it goes, on and on.

*week 7: It has been a very slow and dull week. I did manage to send off a birthday card for one of my relatives. Otherwise it's just reading books and magazines and watching the rain. Dull, dull, dull.

*week 8: It seems to be a very emotional week for the nation. People recovering in Florida from the High School shooting, and the country focusing on the subject of gun laws and mental health issues. It seems that Florida is taking the lead in upping the required age to 21 to purchase any firearm.

While being a supporter of the NRA, I also believe in people being responsible firearm owners. You can't take away the firearms from all the people that are law abiding and leave the criminals and the (now called) "Law Enforcement" with them. We are nearly already a Nazi Germany Police State as it is.

The Federal Government already has "'Big Brother" in the sky and now has around 2,500 surveillance drones in the air above our heads in America at all times, thanks to the National Security Administration. Just like my father told me in the 1970s, "We are voting our rights away."

No more Barney Fife "'peace officers" around anymore; now we have "Law Enforcement." If you get stopped or are a "Person of Interest," they will find something to charge you with so they can justify their existence, and paycheck. Good ol' Uncle Sam and the U.S. of A.

Good Things about Prison

Mostly, inmates don't have any good thoughts about prison. When someone loses their freedom, it is never a good thing to be confined like an animal and have what we assume as our rights taken away from us. But that is just one way to look at it.

There are some inmates who wouldn't have it any other way. These people look at the good side and the advantages that prison life offers them that they can't get in the free world. The following are some of the advantages that they may look at that some of us ignore.

There are educational programs offered. Alcohol and drug education to those that have a dependency problem. In prison, it is offered to a captive audience, whereas in the free world it would be too easy to "slip" and revert back into the old habits of use. A vocational school offers basic education and can lead to a GED for those who want to better themselves when released into the public and have a chance at a job and would perhaps make them a responsible citizen.

There is also a creative writing class that will sharpen and hone the individual's skills at writing and will help them in the free world to be able to explain themselves better and improve their communication skills. For those with a calling, one can obtain a BA in Christian Ministry from New Orleans Baptist Theological Seminary. There are also jobs that a prisoner can get paid for so they have money to buy items at the canteen. These jobs are rare, but it does help with those who are indigent.

Some of the inmates would be homeless upon release. Those individuals would rather stay here where they have shelter and even a "home." They can get their clothes furnished and washed, a bed to sleep on out of the harsh environment. Toiletries furnished, water to wash with if they so choose and even if they don't so choose. Generally three meals a day, a lot of beans, mixed vegetables, instant potatoes, rice, mystery meat, grits, oatmeal, powdered eggs, and watered down coffee. The menu hasn't changed much in the past 50 years. The meals are rarely hot, so there is no chance to burn your tongue or lips.

Then this brings us to the Medical Services. There isn't a whole lot of good to be said of the Medical Treatment that you receive in prison. If it is to their advantage, they will keep you alive. If you complain enough, officials will reluctantly try to see to your needs. No guarantee, though. But they sure will make you suffer a long drawn out time avoiding spending a dime, although it will cost them a dollar to do so.

In conclusion, I do believe that being in prison is somewhat like an old folk's home. Some are better than others. It just depends on how much a person can tolerate and still think happy thoughts. Just goes to show you that one person's Hell is another person's Salvation.

Parchman Christmas

Being that this is my first Christmas in Parchman, but not my first in prison, the setting of the mood is no different from any other facility I've been to. Being kept from your family and friends is always a depressing matter. Seeing the TV news, weather, and holiday commercials adds to the feeling.

Christmas is generally supposed to be for the children, but we all have retained a childlike view of what Christmas is supposed to be. The commercials of Christmas by the retailers have certainly blown all the generations' perception of Christmas as a receiving more than a giving time. There are still a few organizations out there that ask people to give to those who are labeled at poverty level and can't afford the luxury of Christmas.

What we don't see much of is the broadcasting of the true Christmas, the birth of Jesus. Oh sure, they teach it in Sunday School and in the church sermons, but that only reaches the small percentage of us that take the time to attend the services.

I was fortunate enough to have been raised in a church and have embedded in my mind and soul the history of Christmas. This is something I cannot shake off me, even though I've tried in my years of existence. There were times I've doubted the existence of God, but then I have to come back to reality and accept that religion is a basic guideline for people to follow in order to get along with one another.

Don't get me wrong, I had wonderful Christmases growing up, and I presented to my children the usual holiday spirit, so they may also carry on the tradition to their children and hopefully to their children's children as well. But I truthfully enjoy giving presents. Especially to people I know that weren't expecting one from me. It's a kind of a hit-and-run technique I've developed over the years on Christmas and my birthday.

I don't do it to feel superior or to make people feel bad about not giving me a present. But to let them know that, out of the blue, people can show kindness and thoughtfulness and for them to pass it on to others.

Being locked up and out of touch with the people I know, most of whom are dead now, has left a heavy feeling in my heart. In earlier years, it was easier communicating what I wanted to happen. I could still buy presents and have them shipped to their addresses for their birthdays and Christmas and not worry about them buying me anything in return.

Spending Christmas in Parchman is nothing but another day in a life. A boring, sad period to be forgotten as soon as one's mind will allow. Then start looking towards the next one without enthusiasm and wondering if you will be around to experience the dreadful emotions of another year past.

For some of us, this will be the last Christmas they will spend locked up. Either their time will be up, or they'll be paroled, or maybe they'll even be dead, but it will be a past memory of a forgotten one. Hopefully some of them will be reunited with loved ones and friends and will put these memories of here away in the back of their minds.

To all that are in Parchman, I wish you all a Merry Christmas and a Happy New Year. I hope everyone will be healthy and not let the system beat you down. Rules and laws change every day, so there is always hope. That's what Christmas is about: "Hope"!

A Place I Call Home

What I call home is always temporary. Right now, it's at Clinic #31 in Parchman, Mississippi Department of Corrections. I share a 21-½ foot by 21 foot room with five other patient/inmates. We all have single beds, some hospital, others regular iron-frame beds that take two men and a boy to move. The walls are painted an off white, the same as the ceiling that supports six 4-foot fluorescent double-bulb fixtures. There are two wall sconces, also 4-foot fluorescent, that are located on the opposite walls, north and south. The east outside wall houses two iron framed windows with tempered glass to help repel strong blows of force. The floor is of old yellowing 1-foot square tiles that have seen better days in the 1940s.

Roommates are impossible to choose and are usually hard to get along with. One inmate has been in that room for nine years. He has the most to complain about, but does the least amount of complaining. Another is in his mid-eighties and is nearly deaf. He yells when he is speaking. It is always an irritation. A person tries to avoid a conversation with him. A mid-fifties man, recently out of heart surgery and going home soon, has a bad habit of opening the window with the temperature in the 30s and 40s outside, trying to drop the temperature inside to the outside temperature. I have a feeling that eventually the cold will be his downfall.

That leaves the final two roommates. One is easy to get along with and has no irritating habits that stand out. The final one I've known for six years. We were in the same zone at EMCF Meridian, which is a facility that caters to the more mentally handicapped individuals. This one in particular is what people may consider more handicapped than others and definitely not stable enough to be released to the public. I don't see him being here long. He tried to be a resident here before and only lasted five days.

The food here should be a step above the average prison food since we are classified as patients, but it seems to be worse than average slop they have served here for the last fifty years. The same goes for the medical care. Prison medical care has always been substandard, but Parchman medical care has kept with the low-grade medical offering that is nationally known. They will spend that dollar to save that dime. If Corrections would address the medical problems at the time when it comes to their attention, then the worst case scenario would be that the healing process would cost less and be a lot less discomfort for the individual.

By looking out the East Wall windows, you are always reminded of where you are. Just outside our own building is Area #17, where the final moments of an inmate are memorialized with his last breath before the final injection of poison is shot into his system and takes his life as he has taken other lives. Reminds us of where we are and the last hopes of so many before us and the ones that will be after. Brings us back to our drab and dreary room that we call "Home," Parchman MSP, Clinic #31.

Justine Nations

Prison Diary

Tuesday, Jan. 30, 2018
Came back to building J-11 from Creative Writing class. Same ol' same ol'. The news said we're supposed to have a lunar eclipse tonight, well, in the a.m. Maybe we'll get out in time to see it!

Wednesday, Jan. 31, 2018
We didn't' get out until after 6 a.m. this morning. Maybe next time (Eclipse).

Went to the chapel tonight for church. Ma and Pa Morgan from Dublin, TX. Sad when grown folks can't act right in church and the "church people" have to correct them like children. It was very embarrassing to be a part of that crowd! The service was good, though! Leaving the church, I saw a huge full moon! Nice brisk walk back to hell!

Thursday, Feb. 1, 2018
Woke up to all the "Big Wigs" tearing down the women's tents. What good did it do? Nothing. They put them back up as soon as they leave out the door.

I'm feeling kind of depressed. When the po-po comes, I expect things, but they don't change. My bunkie has a tent. Should I say my bunkies? I have two of them. No changes. They tent up clothes lines and have no room except in the "hallway"! No problem until they bitch! And wow do they—mainly with each other—fist fight, curse, yell, and are so disrespectful! Some days, I'm a mess 'cause I'm letting them make me miserable. And today is one of them days! A little country! This being the "throwaway zone," I don't know why the po-po: can't control these people—they are mean, full of hate, disrespectful, only think of themselves!

I'm going to spend time with God, since I'm so negative!

12:45 p.m.

Wow, I started reading the diary of Joseph Dole. We here have no reason to complain. It could be so much worser! (not correct Eng.)

Just got back from supper! I love the fact we have to walk for three meals and two-med calls. It's wonderful, and today it's like spring! That makes me happy. The weather really affects the way I feel! Physically, mentally, and spiritually. Spiritually is what I'm trying to work on these days! Good weather or bad, I need to be spiritually fit all of the time!

Friday, Feb. 2, 2018

Woke up at 6 a.m. for breakfast. It was yucky, and breakfast is my favorite meal! Didn't go to lunch or to the chapel for the play "I am clean." I've seen it before, but I really need to go motivated. Just got back from medication! It's a little nippy outside 'But beautifully Sunny! Rumor—inmate.com says we are going to have an "outing" tomorrow! I'm excited! Back in Nov., they had a softball game with CMCF playing a "real" team! It was great to get out and root for our team! We lost, but we all played nice and it felt real!

Saturday, Feb. 3, 2018

Went to breakfast way before sun-up! Early! Went back to sleep! Woke up in time for lunch. No one knows about our "field-day." Some women are dressing up for the occasion, putting on make-up, doing their hair. I guess for their girlfriends! Ha. I like to get "prettied" up too but not to go sit in the grass! Guess I'm just a party-pooper today! Well, we haven't gone anywhere yet! Finally they called "Yard call!" Three buildings (on yard) and 2A women all together—everywhere from C Building to Gym St. Tyler had hot dogs, popcorn, and juice for everyone! What a nice—cold—few hours! A big prison family reunion. I got to spend time with Heather. I love her so! She loves my Doggie Day Camp idea and 4-S's! We could make mega $$ if we could keep our addictions at bay! That was the excitement for the day, prob. the month.

Sunday, Feb. 4, 2018

Super Bowl Sunday—Woke up to yummy-new smells! These women surely do keep it up for the holidays and special events. I guess the different stuff (garlic-onion) comes from the big kitchen. We never get it! I'm a loner here, not sure why, maybe my age, stingy with what little I do get, not sure. I feel that I'm liked, just not enough to be part of the "crowd"! That's OK too. Maybe if I dressed the part like they do. Not going to happen! I dress for visitation, church. That's about the extent of it! It's not that serious! You can also tell who's HIGH, 'cause they're putting on makeup at 11 pm. It's funny! I still get high on occasion, but I really am working on saying NO, all the time! Getting HIGH is what made me commit crimes! And this (prison) is not where it's at! So I will just be a loner and work on what's in my head! Back to other smells! Yummy foods cooked in a microwave never cease to amaze me! The talent is incredible here—wasted. 10 p.m. The game is over, Philadelphia Eagles won—New England Patriots lost. It was nice to sit and watch the game as a group! Everyone gets along despite the difference in teams and convicts. Well, I'm tired now; going to sleep!

Monday, Feb. 5th

Got a good night's sleep. It's sad that's all that's good right now, but I did go to gym call. It was nice to get out for an hour or so!

Tues., Feb. 6, 2018

Woke up to Pancake Day. Sad when I look forward to food! It's also Canteen Day! Pay my debts and try not to "owe" no more! Looking forward to class! Working on no sleep 'cause of bunkie (yes, two); they rock the bunk, then fight. It's pretty bad!

Wednesday, Feb. 7, 2018

I'm writing this on Thursday. Wednesday was a blah day! Not sure why, except it was raining and my bones (hip and knee) hurt badly.

Thursday, Feb. 8, 2018

Didn't make it to breakfast 'cause I thought it was bologna day, for Anna. Ha! My mistake. I went to lunch anyway, BBQ—"Pork"?

Couldn't gag but a bite down! Get with bow wow. Now I owe her, but it was worth it! Or was it? Ha—I'll learn hopefully one day!

Friday, Feb. 9, 2018
I slept all day!

Sat. Feb. 10, 2018
Visitation Day with Mom is always good but emotionally draining! Got state-issue T-shirts and work shirts. I got cussed out by Lt. L 'cause of Capt. B's saying he'd get me some new shoes. Well, I didn't get any shoes, just my feelings really hurt! Capt. B really turned on me, and Lt. L, got all in my face! I didn't say another word! Big time—Over this Day!

Sunday, Feb. 11, 2018
Woke up so homesick! Guess seeing Mom yesterday didn't help those feelings! Stayed in bed!

Monday, Feb. 12, 2018
?

Tuesday, Feb. 13, 2018
The Day before Valentine's! It's crazy girlfriends, lovers, pillows, outfits, such creativity these women have. If only "we" used the talent before we came in here! I lost $5 today. I should have learned my lesson by now. "It's not worth it." But I'm so miserable. I don't like much—people, food. My life right now suxxx!

Wednesday, Feb. 14, 2018
Valentine's Day, 1989—I married Mike, my kid's daddy! What a mistake divorcing him! It's just one of my many regrets I have. Being an addict and having regrets is not a good combo!

Thursday, Feb. 15, 2018
Wow, this month is flying by! Thank God! Woke up to "Rise and Fly," the $ Spade's tournament! They know how to make the best

of a bad situation! I need to learn from them! Anna Grace went on court order this a.m. I just so happened to wake up and see her leaving! Hopefully everything's gonna be alright. I don't think she was gonna wake me up. It, of course, hurt my feelings. Duh, my feelings are really on my sleeve! My only "friend" has left! "Boohoo," or was she a "friend"? She had four pair of pants in her locker. She said she had 0! That's why I gave her a pair. My new ones Lt. L told me to pack up, is how I found out! Oh well, she must have her reasons! Most of these women have a story, lots of abuse, deception and lies, and a whole lot of criminal activity!

Friday, Feb. 16, 2018
Can't sleep! Obviously no one else can; everyone (not everyone) but a lot of these women are up and going! If they're not putting a needle in their head, they're smoking spice and gating stuck! I know I think I would have been one of those who would have been shooting up, but God has stopped that from happening! I have to thank him daily! I've just got to stop doing suboxone!

Sat., Feb. 17, 2018
Same stuff—different day.

Sunday, February 18, 2018
Called Mom for $ for Saturday. Myra's coming in her place 'cause she'll be out of town! I can't wait.

Mon, February 19, 2018
I'm sick! Put a sick call in!

Tuesday, Feb. 20, 2018
I'm Real Sick!! But I'm going to class!

Richard Henley

Poem

I think of life as I know it
Full of errands and chores
Drive to town and back again
Do a project like I'm on the clock

Swelled up with pride at each completion
I await acknowledgment feeling accomplished
Think of another before my list fades
Can't lose momentum or I'll slip into low

I miss the drudgery of mindless repetition
Resting while seeming to accomplish
Finish each chore just in time
Ready for dinner, funny how that is

Slow day and out of things to do
Good time for missionaries to visit
Offering optimism and rewarding tracts
Out of both at the moment

While I count down the years
In increments that started with days
Crept up to weeks and then months
Went too slow now I count in decades

Not sure I still have a wife
Shouldn't have put her name on the house
Things we do out of love

I miss my dog

Going outside was todays treat
One hour of fresh air and pretense at freedom
Sunlight warms my skin
Enough of this or I may like it

I watch old movies all from my youth
Black and white all shades of gray
Spent years lying on my back
Makes it easier spending hours today

Poem 2

The characters you meet in an enclosed facility
Are as different as black and white
Looks and deficiencies tell their story
Of each man's varied plight

Half are in wheelchairs
Some don't know their own name
But each knows the other's business
In that we are all the same

In a room that sleeps six
You rarely find it complete
Two left some time ago
Leaving four to enjoy their retreat

With one's own dishonesty
He's earned his latest fate
He won't steal from the next guy
But for this time it's too late

On the other side is a bitter pill
Hates everything about life even the weather
Been here two years, nothing improves still
If I leave my torment, I hope we're not together

There are those who wander aimlessly about
They have neither goal nor destination
Their lot is no less important

Than ours which is an abomination

I hope those on the outside
Won't forget me where I am
Letter writing is not everyone's favorite pastime
The distance between communication

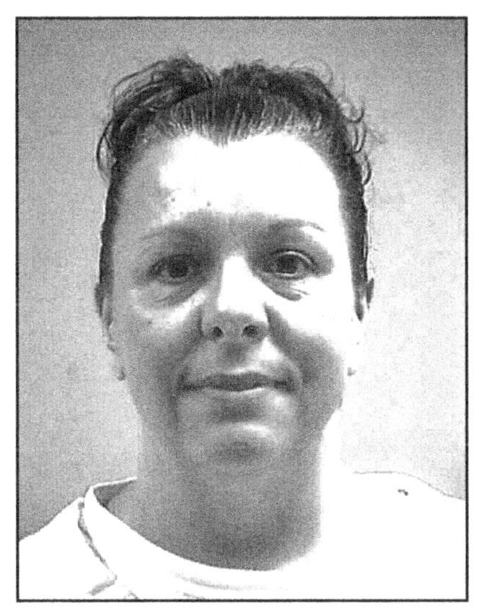

Lori Griffin

Santa Slain

This holiday season, I finally came around a bit and contributed my time and talents to our Disney theme for Christmas. I helped color a few larger than life characters from The Little Mermaid and Beauty and the Beast. I also created a geometric design on the floor to mimic the ballroom scene where Belle and the Beast dance under the chandelier. The reason I've been reluctant to do this stems from my second Christmas in prison here in Mississippi.

In 2014 our zone brought forth its residents' talents and artistic abilities along with a resourceful creativeness. Against the wall in the back of the zone, we had an 8-foot-tall Santa at the fireplace with the stockings hung, and a fully decorated tree behind him. All drawn by hand on poster paper, displaying exquisite talent. It was a scene reminiscent of the classic M&M candies commercials for Christmas, where the M&Ms faint when they see Santa nibbling on cookies and depositing presents under the tree, shouting: "He is real!"

It was a talented masterpiece that brought joy and excitement for the holidays to many in a place that is filled with grim holiday dinners and desperately needed basic necessities as holiday gifts. This year's Thanksgiving Dinner was a dismal meal of frozen turkey slices with ice crystals still glistening from its texture, spoiled chicken used in the cornbread chicken and dressing, a half-baked roll still raw in the middle, green beans with no salt and pepper for seasoning, and for dessert, a small square of white sheet cake with no icing. And there was absolutely nothing to drink to choke it all down with, as is the norm in the 2A dining hall when it comes to having a beverage with our meals. And I expect no different for our Christmas Meal either, along with our Christmas gift bags of socks, shampoo, and hopefully deodorant. These things the state does not provide for inmates who are considered indigent like myself. So a bottle of shampoo to stretch over a year's time, along with deodorant that never lasts more than a month, and socks that actually fit are truly a blessing here in the Mississippi Prison System. But I'm guessing if most found these presents under their tree as gifts from Santa, they would wonder why they were on his naughty list and what they had done to offend the Jolly Man. Me, I'm smiling ear from ear anxiously awaiting the donation by the church of these items.

But what really broke my spirit for celebrating the holiday season in 2014 were the unforgettable events that took place on that Christmas Eve. Everyone in the Zone was full of glee and cheerful anticipation of the holiday. Then it all changed in a blink of an eye. 2B-Zone was raided by the K9 unit that Christmas Eve. They came in military strike fashion, dressed in camouflage and bullet-proof vests, and began immediately implementing a Reign of Terror. They started hastily in a violent whirlwind tearing down all of our Christmas decorations from the walls.

Santa was assaulted and torn from his post by the fireplace. The tree was chopped down and dissected limb from limb with all its trimmings, while Santa was dismembered and his remains were thrown to the floor in shattered pieces. It looked like a grotesque murder scene. Santa lay slain on the floor. It was enough to break anyone's spirit who had ever loved the festivities of the holiday season. In prison or not.

The events of that Christmas Eve have stuck with me these years. I haven't wanted any part of decorating for the holidays since then.

But ultimately the goal of this article is to shed light on the downtrodden women here in the Mississippi Prison System and the constant disappointments they face on a daily basis. And why classes like this one that focus our attention on creative writing are so important and why they need to continue and expand. These classes are desperately needed; the average inmate has between a third and seventh grade education. But the classes are not only educational; they offer a psychological benefit as well. They are a mental release for thoughts and emotions in a controlled environment, especially when true mental health counseling is missing for the mass incarcerated.

Classes like this one break up the monotony of the sedentary lifestyle women suffer here in the Mississippi Prison System. A world where 132 women live in one room, 2.5 feet apart from one another's beds, with only 36 seats in the common areas, encourages the women to lie in bed all day. With the lack of jobs on the compound and Educational Programs being restricted and limited, support for classes such as this one is needed to make a positive change and improvement in those women's lives.

Many are unaware that in the state of Mississippi the prison recidivism rate is 85%, while the state of New York, which incorporates the infamous Riker's Island prison, has a recidivism rate of only around 45%. The DOJ predicts that the rate of women in prison will increase annually by 3% nationwide. New York State partnered with local colleges and introduced classes to its prison population that actually offer degrees. With this program, its recidivism rate declined to around 18% for those who attended the classes. Providing true education is key to breaking the cycle of poverty and criminal behavior often associated with the desperation of poverty. These classes work, and they need your support. As the Bible quotes in the New Testament, Matthew 25:42: "Remember the prisoner." They are in turmoil and desperate for love and understanding. And education in all forms, including the arts, helps the prisoner cope and realize there is love in the world. This is why your support is needed.

Comforts in Prison

Comfort in prison is an oxymoron. The lack of the simplest comforts in prison is immense. It ranges from scalding hot shower water that can't be tempered to ice cold food that suffers from a lack of seasoning. Comforts like air conditioning in the sweltering heat of the tropical summers in Mississippi or a pillow to rest your head on at night are non-existent. Those are comforts that prison life does not afford me. But what comfort prison does give me is the comfort of time. Since I was afforded the luxury of time with a 20-year prison sentence, I have tried to take advantage of it. In the last five years I have learned to read and write Arabic on a rudimentary level and have gone through prisoner's law school. Over the years, I've dabbled in other interests, like language skills in German and Spanish, and learning about alternative energy resources for solar farms, wind turbines, and urban farming. But truly the only comfort I've had while being in prison was the comfort of a man. We would see each other occasionally and write to each other as regularly as possible. This man offered me a comfort that many don't have in their Prison Life. I was and am very thankful for his support over the years. He gave me the comfort of having someone to share my thoughts with, and he would tell me he loved me. That comfort meant the most to me, and I will always remember it.

Anthony Bell

Prison Journal

Monday Dec 30, 2019

Found out this morning we were on a statewide lockdown! Whoopee! Nobody knows why. Speculation is they don't have any help. That makes sense. I don't mind the lockdown. My concern is—I have a TV on order. They've taken the money off my books for the TV. If we're on lockdown, they won't get my TV this week if they don't pass out canteen because of the lockdown. I need some laundry done! Won't happen if we're on lockdown. I got one more shirt—I need a shower—What do I do? Oops—wrong! I'm out of clean shirts! I would have to put on a dirty shirt—they picked up the laundry! But they're not going to wash it until tomorrow.

Tuesday Dec. 31, 2019

New Year's Eve—They told me to get ready to go to the cancer clinic—then said that was probably a mistake, that I was going to see the doctor here. I hope they do laundry. I hope they pass out canteen this week—I would sure like to get my TV! Breakfast was light—but—praise God for what I got! I have some milk, and I'll have some cereal after med-care. They wanted me to go to 42 and get two units of blood, but they hadn't even checked my levels! When they checked them, I didn't need any blood.

Wednesday Jan 1, 2020

Happy New Year—Nothing exciting happened. No special food. Had a riot—three killed. Bad things all the way around. It's all over the news.

Thursday Jan 2, 2020

I wish I had my TV. On lockdown—can't go to Day Room and watch TV or get a book from day room or library. Bored. Called Tab and Anita. Don't have much left in my locker to eat. Hope we get canteen soon!

Friday Jan 3, 2020

Still on lock down—100 MS Highway patrolmen and helicopter; two escaped. I have no doubt they will find them. The Lord moved me from 30 to 31 just in time! This place (31) is a good place—but—lots about Marshall County better or as good. Sure wish we would get canteen! It would be nice to have my TV and my canteen order. Got my TV stand, and I'm ready to go.

Saturday Jan 4, 2020

Nothing special today—lots of rumors and stories about lockdown going around. Not sure what to believe. Everybody thinks they have the real story. Talk to Anita and Tab often. It lifts me up to hear their voices. Praise God they took the laundry—but didn't wash it. I'll have to start washing some clothes when I'm in the shower. Maybe next week some things will change—I hope so.

Sunday Jan 5, 2020

Started reading my Bible again—about time, huh? I have really ignored the Lord since I've been in Parchman. Got to get back, close to God. I realized I was putting canteen before God! I gotta fix that—Wow, raunchy supper! I'm starting to run low on coffee.

Monday Jan 6, 2020

I've been up all night with diarrhea. My stomach's been cramping. They told me I had to go to sick call. That was supposed to be cancelled. I asked the Nurse here—she checked and said I don't have to go. Hope we get canteen today! We were supposed to start our creative writing class this morning, but the lockdown stopped that.

Tuesday Jan 7, 2020
Went to Greenwood and got cancer treatment—this is the long one. Went well. Doctor said my blood count was very good. One of the drivers got us in and out of 42 quickly! Got back to 31 and crashed.

Wednesday Jan 8, 2020
Was supposed to go to Greenwood—I thought. But got sent to 42 instead—I hate going there! Waited for four hours to see a doctor. When I told them I wanted to sign a refusal, then all of a sudden it was time for me to see the doctor. Saw Ms. Brown. Told her the good news about my blood and got some Excedrin and went to 31. Canteen people put all the $ back on my books except the $ for the TV and remote—so I placed a big order. Don't know when we'll get off lockdown. Maybe they will go ahead and give me my TV. My appetite has come back. Won't be able to keep my milk deal up much longer. Maybe I'll get taken to Greenwood Thursday. Going to 42 today was a waste. I've learned that what made MCCF so great was the people—Bogan, Chris, Ray, Brian, Jesse, etc.—Miss ya guys.

Thursday Jan 9, 2020
Well I didn't go to Greenwood today. I need my other chemo treatment. That's why I'm at Parchman—not because I want to be! A bus left out of here this morning—don't know what's going on exactly. When is this lockdown gonna end! I called canteen—they didn't take the $ off my books for the order I placed yesterday. I wish they would give me my TV. I have a bag of coffee left. I'll have to count my noodles and juice.

Friday Jan 10, 2020 Storm!
Heard a rumor of Feb. 3—but it was inmate.com. I'm hungry all the time. Not enough food. Richard is having trouble breathing—taking him to the hospital. I prayed for him. I have two books and four papers to read. I'm gonna take my time with the papers—probably take all weekend with 'em. Time to read my Bible—no power—no water.

Saturday Jan 11, 2020

Storm went thru last night—they didn't get emergency generator on till the sun came up. After an hour or so, it went off. They have it back on, but no hot water. Wish they would get the power restored—I would like to microwave a cup of coffee. Lord help me to like it here because I don't! Can't help but wish I was at Marshall County. No power—no water—can't flush.

Sunday Jan 12, 2020

No power—no water—can't flush or shower. The toilets are overflowing. We don't have any water to drink—we have limited electricity with a small generator. Our food is limited. Supper last night was a salami sandwich, four cookies, and a serving of pineapple. Guard said they were supposed to bring us some bottled water yesterday, but they didn't. This place is a mess. The only reason I'm here is to get my chemo—Marshall County was so much better than here. I miss Marshall County and my friends there. This is the best place I can be right now. God is in charge—I have to remember that and rely on Him, not depend on man or canteen or anything else of this world.

Monday Jan 13, 2020

The power came back on. Then it went off again after breakfast, and we went back on the generator. I guess the utility company is still working on it. We do have water, and I took a shower this morning. I feel better. We had cereal, eggs, sausage, and tortillas for breakfast this morning—It was good! Lots of bad attitudes and people who hate everything and everybody in Unit 31. Not a lot of people I care to get to know or become friends with here. Hope I can pick up the game tonight on my radio. I wish they would let me have my TV—they took the money for it! I'm so hungry. If we don't have much for lunch, I'm gonna fix a noodle. Gotta put together a canteen order today. The power is flickering again! I'm not going to use but one more piece of paper on this journal.

Tuesday Jan 14, 2020

I got my TV! But they didn't bring my remote. I love the TV. The food is getting back to normal.

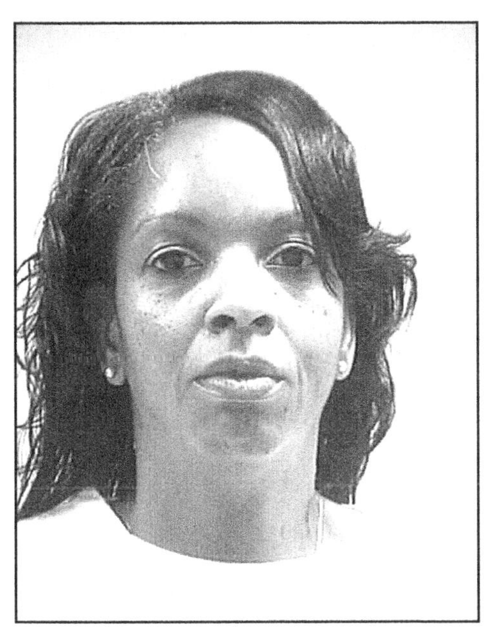

Patricia Hall

X-Mas Behind Bars

I thought I was living the Life. The life I'd always dreamed of. Growing up, my family watched a lot of movies with Brown Sugar, Dolomite, etc. The movies always had house parties that were filled with pimps, prostitutes, hustlers, and drugs. For some reason, this fascinated me. I was blown away by the money, cars, fine clothes,- and the attention. The beauty of being the "number one chick" was more than I dreamed of, or so I thought. Little did I know all of the crippling requirements that followed.

The pimp I met became my husband in a matter of days. I thought becoming his wife meant no more working in the streets. No more sexual favors for financial benefits. God knows, I was so tired of living that life. My mind and heart was made up. Since I'd gotten married, I'd spend my days and nights with my children. It was now X-Mas time. I told my husband, I no longer wanted to live that life, full of sex, drugs, and lies. He informed me that there was no escaping; I was now his wife. He told me, I am your pimp, and a real pimp pimps his wife. I explained to him how I wanted to give my life to Christ. What better X-Mas gift could I give God than devoting all my love and time to Him and my children?

I tried to run' I tried to hide, from that life I refuse to live. The more I refused, the more he made me realize what he said was true. There's no escaping his Wrath. I was tortured by day. I was pimped by night. With X-Mas being only days away, my heart was so full of hurt and pain, all I could do was pray. The money was made, the bills were paid, and all the presents were beneath the tree. I'm caught up in this web; I'm bound with chains. I couldn't understand the feelings I felt, nor did I want the hand I was dealt. I'm crying out for mercy—please free me, Lord—for this was my "Christmas Behind Bars."

This is proof you don't have to be in prison to have a X-mas Behind Bars.

DAY ONE OF FOREVER

Today is my first day of keeping a journal. I was asked by my teacher to write something every day. Well, I really didn't like to write, and I feel as if I don't have the time to write. I've been at work pretty much all day, doing hair and nails. The time is now 4:59 p.m.; closing is supposed to be at 5:00 p.m. I'm sure we'll be here 'til whenever the last client hair dries enough to go out in the cold. Today has been a pretty good day for me. My mind and thoughts are pretty much all over the place. I'm thinking about how tired I am of doing time. I've been incarcerated for 23 years now, and counting. The Man says I have 27 more years to go before I become a free citizen again. Lately, I've been fearing going back to court. After serving 17 years of my sentence, God put someone in my life that saw and felt like I deserved another chance at Freedom. She paid $10,000 in full for me to get an attorney. My attorney has been working on my case for nearly two years. She has to interview the main witness in my case on Feb. 23, 2018. Then she will start filing the paperwork. I was sentenced to 50 habitual years for armed robbery, plus 20 for aggravated assault. The aggravated assault charge is run concurrent with the 50. No one was killed in this crime. Thank God. However, with the way the Judicial System is here in Mississippi, I would've gotten less time had I killed him. Yes, you read it correctly. Mississippi doesn't value a person's life. You kill someone, you plead out to manslaughter and get 20 years. However, you'd only serve 10 years or less. In case you didn't know, Mississippi is still burning. It's prejudiced as hell. Yes, the Ku Klux Klan still exists. They are all over the world—especially here in Mississippi. All twelve jurors were Caucasian. This is to also include all court officials. I couldn't afford an attorney, so one was appointed to me. I had a noose around my neck before my trial even started.

Anyway, as my attorney prepares my paperwork, reality sets in. If I'm granted a new trial, there are no guarantees that I will get time served. They could give me the same amount of time again or even more. Not to mention, I must relive that whole scene over again. I'm afraid of the unknown. You'd think after serving 23 years here—I should be able to handle whatever comes my way. Well, I don't think I can. I'm so tired. I've held on to my faith, my hope since the beginning. My strength is getting weaker; I'm getting older. Reality is, I can die here. That's not what I want, nor do I want to believe that. However, Death is someone everyone will face. There's no escaping it. No one but God knows our due date. I just pray God will bless me, show me favor, and give me the chance to reunite with my family before my day comes. Give me plenty of years to be with my children, grandchildren, mother, and my siblings.

Kenneth Dennis

Time Passing

I have gone through my span of Life. I was given birth from my mother's womb, learned how to talk and walk, learned my ABCs, and eventually learned how to read and write. I learned Right from Wrong, and still I wind up serving time in the Mississippi State Penitentiary. I am trying to be strong.

As I reflect back on the time span of my life, I realize time is really passing. Time is passing by at a much quicker rate than I could ever fathom. What's really so pathetic about time passing is, I am still serving this life sentence in the Mississippi State Penitentiary.

Looking Out

While looking out the Prison Window, I see cars and trucks constantly going up and down the highway. Highway 49 is right outside my window view. Miles away, though.

The people driving these vehicles have no idea I'm watching them travel up and down the highway, as I'm looking out the prison window.

Everybody is going about their lives, and when they've finally reached their destination, be it home or wherever, they still won't know I saw them driving by while I was looking out the Prison Window and yearning for my freedom.

In the Middle of the Night

Once I go to sleep at night,
I toss and turn like I'm in a fight
Every night I lose my sight to sleep,
I pray that I may still have my right to weep.

How It Is

There's only one way I know how to begin telling anyone about life in prison. I have to tell it as I've lived my life in prison for the last 33-½ years.

My life in prison hasn't been all good. It's been terrible, to be honest. I've had some brief moments when I didn't feel I was confined. Although, it was drug induced, and when off the drugs, the problem of still being here was forever present afterwards.

Anyway, I've seen practically everything there is to be seen in prison. I've seen some messed up stuff and seen some pretty decent acts of kindness.

Actually, it's hard to really detail events. However, I'm going to try to tell about a couple of events I've personally witnessed that have stayed on my mind throughout my stay since they happened.

One was a stabbing that happened while I was at 24 ext. in the 80s. The reason it's stayed on my mind so long is, it happened right over my head. I was playing dominoes, and the two guys came out of their room almost simultaneously. One was black; the other was white. The black guy was in front of the white guy, when all of a sudden, I heard a knife going into flesh. I turned my head, and I saw this guy running to the door trying to pull a knife from his back. I heard another guy (the white guy) say: "Now take that!" All of that stemmed from the black guy taking $20 from the white guy. Was it worth it? Hell, no!

That's one instance where prison is really messed up and no one stepped in to make the situation better.

When I was locked down at Unit 32, in 1994, I became very sick. My sugar level had gotten pretty high. I barely was able to talk. Anyway, I made it to my cell door some kind of a way and was able to get the attention of the guy in the cell next to me. I told him I was sick, and he got the attention of everyone on the cell block. They all began beating above their cells until finally a guard came up to the cell block and asked what the problem was. I told him I didn't feel well, and he got me to the clinic. That's where it was discovered my sugar level was too high.

If it wasn't for the guys on the cell block, I'd probably would have died. I stayed in the hospital eight days behind that. But the good thing was how all these guys banded together to make sure I got medical attention.

There's been way more chilling events that have happened since I've been here. However, I'm narrating this narrative in a rush. I'll probably be asked to add on. If so, there's more that has stayed with me since I've seen them.

Prison Life isn't anything nice, but it's survivable. Mostly it's a matter of minding your own business.

If I had only listened to my mom when I was a child.

Stay in school and not be wild.

Get a job and not steal.

Things would probably be a whole lot different than what they are now.

I'm always wondering: if I had listened to my mom when I was a child.

I have seen the good, the bad, and the ugly.

I have seen the good, when I saw a bunch of guys come together to save another man's life.

I have seen the bad when I saw a bunch of guys beat to death another man.

I have seen the ugly when one man let loose his last gasp of life before death overcame him.

I have seen the good, the bad, the ugly.

Eyes Wide Open to My Captivity

In prison, you must keep your eyes wide open.

There's always some game coming from all directions. From the east, west, the north, and south. So in order to be able to see the game coming at you, you have to keep your eyes as well as your brain wide open…

It's very harmful if one shuts their eyes and closes their brain to the happenings surrounding them.

It's not saying participate in what's going on around, but be aware that they're going on.

The title of this writing is "Captivity." I'm titling it this because of the condition I feel right now as I'm confined in prison.

Webster's Dictionary defined captivity as "the state or condition of being held captive esp., in war." I'm not at war with anyone, but I feel constantly I'm warring with my inner self.

In all truth, though, my feeling of captivity stems from years and years of constant confinement in Mississippi State Penitentiary at Parchman. Actually, my whole being feels in captivity, because it's a constant thought, because I'm so vividly reminded of my Captivity. The walls, bars, and concrete and steel are my reminders.

My name is Kenneth Dennis. I've served in prison 33-½ years of my 62 years of life. I've seen quite a lot. I've witnessed personally this prison crumble. Not only has it crumbled in building deterioration but also in deterioration of the System of Rehabilitation. The whole prison control and structural quality has fallen down.

It's truly amazing how much this prison has changed. When I first came here, this prison made money and so did the inmates. Now everybody sits around and watches everybody and everything fall to pieces.

Lately, I've discovered my condition varies. It goes from bearable but unpleasant to downright disgusting! These changes happen within a flash or a heartbeat. I've learned to adjust to it.

People, places, and things are normally the three elements that control the conditions of prison confinement. That's been my perception since my confinement.

People, including the inmates, security personnel, the administrative staff, the commissioner, etc., all the people included in running a prison have different personalities and opinions. I was once told by an officer who worked his way up from a regular correctional officer to a Warden that to run a prison effectively, the prisoners must be involved in the decisions regarding their rehabilitations and their programs here while in prison.

Prison Life—when I first came here—was so much easier. We had incentives to work for. We realized our visits were privileges, for those who were married, their conjugal visits, our packages, etc. These incentives may have seemed small to someone looking in, but for us who were actually living our lives here, they made life a lot more bearable. We are basically discussing things now that made my life so much easier then than now.

But, in all truth, life and the things I go through now aren't all that bad for being in prison. To be honest, it's the housing unit. Unit 31 is so much different than the other units. Now, if I was a smoker, doper, gambler, or any of the other bad vices one could involve themselves in while in prison, I'd be bored to death and would have to leave here as soon as possible. Since I'm not into those vices anymore, I'm able to deal with what goes on here. There are sick men here. There are guys who have been here a long time. Since I'm not in the best of health myself, I do good, and I get along with the Security Staff.

I came here March 23, 2018 to go under observation for recovery from congestive heart failure. They prescribed me blood thinners that had to be passed out by the nurse. At first, I wanted to go back to Unit 30 where I came from before I had my heart attack. After a while, I realized that I hadn't completely recovered. There were still things wrong with me, and I wouldn't want to be in general population environment like Unit 30 with these problems. So 3-L was cool for now. As time progressed, so did I. I started helping in the building and upkeep, and eventually, once I got discharged, I got hired as camp support. That was in August 2018.

Still, captivity hasn't been easy. On January 15, 2019, I received another five years set off. That was devastating. We all should have some hope when we've been in captivity for so long at being free one day. It is not men's nature to be confined such as this. So, I felt let down. However, I knew I still had to carry on. My family, my mom, brother, and other relatives were hoping also for me to become free this time. I had done 13 years of set offs. So yes, five years more was hard to accept. However, that's what I had to do, because unless these folks would reconsider, after reading my reconsiderations, I would be stuck for the five years, if not die here. And that's what I don't want to do. I don't want to die in prison. Now that does worry me. Regardless, though. I have to carry on.

This writing has been complicated for me because I'm going through some personal stuff that seems to overwhelm me at times. Finally, I was able to gather my thoughts and came to this much of a story. There's more, but I can't say much more than this. My life seems to flash by in little glimpses. Although some of the experiences I have had in and out of prison, I'd rather forget than share with anyone. My life hasn't been pretty or a Bed of Roses. But the new beginning which started years ago gives me a lot to look forward to. With me quitting drugs, alcohol, gambling, and smoking cigs and in accepting Islam as my way of life. I'm looking forward to practicing this way of life in the Free World. In prison, we're watered down by the establishment.

The Sun Is Shining

It's a beautiful day outside, but because of my situation, I am confined to my cell.

Lord, how I wish I could feel the radiant rays of the sun on my skin. The sun is shining bright, and I know it feels right. The sun is life refurbishing itself. It heals the bones that has ached all winter long. It turns the grass green after a long hard rain. I can go on and on about the sun when it is shining. However, I'm going to leave you with what I've already said about the sun when it is shining and with your own thoughts about the sun when it's shining down on you.

Growing Up in the Ghetto

The first 11 or so years of my life, I'd grown up in Bayou August Homes, one of several sub-housing projects in East Biloxi, smack dab in the middle of the ghetto, and this is where my earliest memories begin. My family, as well as every other Black and Vietnamese family who lived there, lived on government assistance, on Welfare and Medicare. Ever since I can remember, I'd always had free lunch in school. So did all my Vietnamese peers. Because if you were wealthy, you wouldn't be living in the projects, nor would you get Welfare and Medicare assistance.

Each project has its own uniqueness, and what set Bayou August Homes apart from other sub-housing apartments was what we called the "Bayview Bridge"—a 20-foot catwalk across a concrete bridge to the Bayview Homes, the adjacent project. Bayou August loosely means "majestic creek" but the Bayview Bridge was anything but majestic! The concrete bridge was sturdy and structurally sound by any means; however, the creek itself was polluted. Everybody threw trash in the creek. I remember litter, bicycle frames and tires, along with the filth and general uncleanliness of the area.

Bayou August Homes indeed!

But it wasn't all negative, my childhood memories of Bayou August Homes. I was an innocent child in the '80s when my family, who had migrated from Vietnam after the fall of Saigon lived there. I could remember walking to Gorenflo Elementary every morning, me and about 80 other Vietnamese kids, out the back iron fence gate of Bayou August Homes. It was a mere two blocks, with a big church on the corner of Lameuse St. and a police officer directing traffic. I've never heard or known of a child, whether Black or Vietnamese, being abducted on the way to school, although looking back, it could well have happened. Eighty-plus children, no parents to walk with them or to look after them, walking out of an apartment back gate two blocks to reach Gorenflo Elementary School. The possibility exists...But as I said, we were innocent children, walking to an innocent school. I could go on and on about Gorenflo Elementary. I did get a certificate for being one of those students who completed his entire K-5 grade levels at one school—but there was nothing out of the ordinary at Gorenflo and it doesn't warrant further discussion.

I remember the good and bad things about living in the Projects. There were the drugs and prostitution—needles and condoms scattered about the parking lot. I once saw a hoopty hopping up and down at night, with people inside, although I was too young to realize what was going on. I once saw a Black woman getting into a fight with a Black man in the parking lot. He reached out and tore her t-shirt and bra, leaving her breasts dangling as she tried to hit him with his clubbed fists. I must've been eight years old or so.

I used to hate this but am smiling inwardly as I think about it—a handful or a dozen of my Vietnamese friends, it makes no difference, playing in the playground for Bayou August Homes when another group of Black kids, mostly older, who would come and some very nasty fights would break out indeed.

I've lived around Black people my entire life, have even been babysat by Black women while my parents were at work in one of the Biloxi Back Bay's many seafood factories, and I can assert that they are not bad people. They were just like the Vietnamese. We all were just trying to make the best of our given situation. There's nothing wrong about that. I remember this one elderly Black woman whom my adolescent friends and I called "the freezing cup woman." We didn't even know her name; all we knew was that she sold frozen juice cups for 25 cents each. That was a lot of $ in the '80s, 25 cents. And I don't know how any of us Viet kids did it, but we'd find a quarter or two and we'd knock on this Black woman's door. When she answered, we'd produce the quarter and hand it to her, telling her we'd like to buy a "freezing cup," as it was called. This wizened elderly woman made a fortune out of us kids in those days, ha ha....

My parents never bought any toys for my brothers and me, but each Xmas, we'd go down to City Hall with gift vouchers to get free toys donated to us by the Veteran's Association. They gave gift cards to low-income families, such as those who lived in housing homes, and we'd go down to City Hall, wait in line with other Black and Vietnamese parents on Christmas morning to collect our donated toys. Every little boy used to get a rubber basketball and, depending on age, would also receive scooters or bicycles. I received a bicycle one time, towards the end of one of the last year or two of receiving these free Christmas toys. I was the happiest kid in the projects! I rode my bicycle every day, for about a week, right in front of Apt. #107 where my parents could see me. I remember parking the bike right in front of Apt. 107's door and going inside for a cold glass of water, and when I came back out, less than five minutes later, my bike was gone! Some thief done took it inside their apartment, stealing the best X-mas present I ever had.

I've known poverty since I was born and lived in Bayou August Homes. Although I was completely devastated when my bike was stolen, ruining my Christmas that year, looking back on it, I don't hold no ill will towards whoever stole my bike. All of us were poor denizens in Bayou August Homes.

Last I heard, Bayou August Homes and several other projects were being demolished to make room for newer apartments.

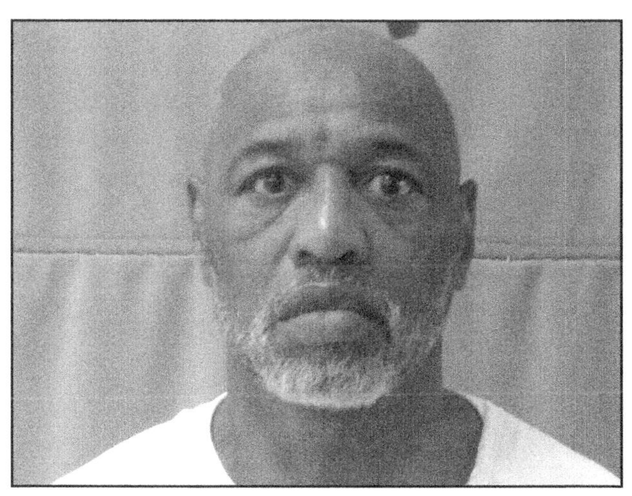

Arthur Gentry

2020 Darkness of Dark

It all began 40 years ago when I received a life sentence to the Mississippi State Penitentiary at Parchman. Little did I know that, when the first thing to beat me there was the head lights of the police car, I was going to live a life of Total Darkness.

April 1980, the second day of the month, I was brought to the R&D which was called the Vocation Center at the time. Everyone was placed in holding cells waiting for their name to be called so that they could be processed in the penitentiary. Once your name was called, you were fingerprinted and asked your name and date of birth, your shoe size, your clothes size, and your weight and height. You then waited for clothes to be given to you and got a haircut, which was a balled head, followed by a mug shot, which is a picture I.D. The things you got included pants, shirts, t-shirts, and boxer's shorts, pillowcase, and two sheets. Then we were shown to a rank where we were to stay a week to two weeks before being transferred to where we will spend our Incarcerate Life. Welcome to the World of Dark.

I was told to pack my belongs and get on to the prison van that was to take me to Camp 4, where I was to be housed for my time at Parchman. April 29, 1980 was my first day at Camp 4, where I was assigned a bed and locker box, given a spoon, and left to myself. I heard talk, little talk, around me of new meat, which I got that night. If I say I was not scared, I'll be lying through my teeth. I put my few belongings in my box, sat around, watched TV, staying to myself and watching everything and everybody around me. I was really scared shitless, not wanting to go to the restroom, which I needed to do badly and which I finally did. As I was walking to the bathroom, I could hear guys whispering about me. Right then I knew I was going to have a problem. I told myself to get ready. I did not know anyone, and I refused to be taken advantage of in any kind of way. So I said to myself that by any way necessary I was going to protect myself. Later on that day, the door was opened and everyone was allowed to go out on the yard, which I did. Some guys were playing basketball, some volleyball, some horseshoes, and others lifting weights or other things. I asked the guys who were lifting weight could I join them. I was given a yes, so that's how I spent the day. When yard call ended, everybody returned to their own respectful zone to do their own things. You had to get in line for the shower, so I got in place and waited my turn. Well, while I was waiting my turn for a shower, guys came up to me for conversation, asking several questions and such, some offering advice and asking could they help me in any way. But this one older guy told me that a young guy should take nothing from nobody for nothing is free. They always expect something back.

So my time finally came for a shower. I gathered my things and walked down the alleyway toward the shower when I heard remarks and whispering. I stopped and looked the way it was coming, but it stopped. So I went on to the shower and showered. This time I knew who it was, so I went and got dressed, and then went back to the bathroom where I saw a mop bucket. I pushed the bucket down the alleyway 'til I got to the group of guys that was talking. I then grasped the ringer out of the bucket and hit this one guy dead in the face. Blood immediately started to run from his face as I hit him repeatedly before I felt guys grabbing me, pulling me back. The officer opened the door, screaming, "Everyone return to your damn racks, except for you, young man. Stand right where you are." He searched me down and handcuffed me, sending me to stand in the hallway. I heard him talking with the guys on the zone a few minutes later.

Officer Walker, I later found out his name to be, informed me that he had to move me across the hall because I'd been in an altercation and could not be housed on the same zone with this guy they call "Truck." I was written a Rule Violation Report for fighting in self-defense.

The guy Truck was taken to the hospital from Camp 4 for medical attention and brought back that same night. The next day after count that morning, yard call was called which I also later found out was every day from 8 to 1, which was feeding time, and then from 2 to 1 each day, if weather permitted it. So I got up for breakfast and was informed by the guy that I had to be up and dressed by 8 with my bed made, but could then lay back down. On the yard, guys began to come to me giving me the lowdown on the way of the penitentiary. So that day I played basketball and walked the recreation area. Throughout the day, I did other things, such as play cards and dominoes. It soon spread around the camp that Young Tex would fight and did not take no shit. That was the name they gave me: Young Tex.

After my first day's experience, things ran smoothly for me, and I made friends but basically stayed to myself as much as possible.

The week passed by slowly with the same things happening day in day out: playing cards, dominos, going to the yard, and watching TV. As the weekends came around, you saw a lot of girl boys washing clothes and ironing, and as night came, you saw more tents going up and guys going behind them with boys.

During the weekends, I learned you stayed up all night and that was when everybody did their thing. But Saturday night was the night they watched Soul Train and f_ _ ked all night. The gay boys danced on table and made their money if they did not have a regular man, but if one had a man, he was off limits. They had lipstick and homemade gowns, and they would smoke weed and drunk homemade beer with the guys that had it. On Sunday, you'd go to visitation, and friends could visit with you for five hours, 9–2 o'clock. I lived this kind of life for two years here at Camp 4, watching and witnessing guys getting raped and stabbed. You name it, it happened. Guys gambled every day and there were fights and stabbings all the time. On visiting Sundays, there were a lot of women coming to visit, which I later learned were whores who got paid good for sex in the tank room that was used for guys who was married. Then there was a selection in the back of the zone that was off limits, for guys who bought sex that was set up by the floor walkers who got paid along with the officer. There was drinking and smoking of weed all throughout visitation each week. If you had money, you could get anything you wanted as long as you kept your mouth closed and stayed out of trouble.

If you were not scared and could hold up for yourself, you got turned onto things that were happening around the camp. After being there for three months, I got involved with the Money Order Scam, first by writing letters for guys and letting them use my name to catch money and write checks. Every letter I wrote or letter written in my name, I got 100 dollars, and then I got to doing the money orders myself. I was making $3,500 and sometimes more a week, and that was not counting the money I was making from gambling and drugs.

And honestly speaking, young white boys coming into the system at a young age did not stand a chance. Most white guys had well-off families and compassionate parents who was very caring, whereas their son was of concern. Most of these people were used. It was not "gang related" back then, but it was territory or what was called home boys. So even back then, it was the organization who ruled things.

We the prisoners are always wrong and blamed for everything but in all actuality, the staff are always involved one way or another. Because like it is said, money is the root of all evil and corruption. That's one of the reasons they took money out of the system, but that did not change anything. It just made us get smarter. I eventually left Camp 4, because I got in a fight and went to the hole, as we call it, which is lockdown. I stayed in lockdown for two weeks waiting disciplinary action to determine my guilt or innocence. I was found not guilty and sent to Camp 23, where I went to school. I got in school and took ABE because all the trade classes were full, but I was put on the waiting list. This was a whole new experience and more relaxing. I got on the boxing team and baseball team, so I had a lot to do to kill time. I stayed at Unit 23 for five years and ended up getting a degree in carpentry, and also started in sheet metal.

All My Children

I've lived 39 years of my adult life in the state penitentiary here at Parchman, and I've learned the uniqueness of the essence of Christmas. From the beginning we are all God's Children, and for that reason, God gave us his only begotten Son.

Now let's try to remember that Christmas is not all about sharing presents and having lavish BBQ parties with family and friends. But it is about giving and sharing the love of God with all his children, and, yes, Christmas is a good time of year.

From the beginning we as men were put on earth to be in control of all things and bowing to the Will of God Almighty.

To sit here in prison watching talk shows and GMA video tapes and pictures of family and friends, BBQing and enjoying it to the fullest, gives me the blues. But yet I am happy for the joy of life and the reason for this season and to share the "Good News." God is alive and real this very day. Grace and mercy. All can be saved.

I have no presents and no family to share them, but all you friends to share my love. Oh, what a blessed Christmas. Thanks for giving us love.

Kids and grandkids I cannot give even a hug and warm kiss. God almighty knows I am truly blessed. Oh, yes, it would be wonderful to see my little ones' faces light up as they open presents, running in the house screaming and hollering from the toys and other things they have received, but here my Christmas is as quiet as a mouse creeping through the house.

Can my Christmas get any worse? Sure it can. K-9 bust interrupting a joyful and happy time we're sharing. Screaming "MFs, hit the floor. No one move." Merry Christmas. Feel the blues. K-9 dogs running through the zones jumping on beds and shitting on them.

The K-9 officers laughing and making jokes. The K-9 commander shouts, "Everybody, let's get out of here. These broke down niggers ain't got nothing. Let's go." So as they exit, the zone commander calls me, "Gentry, there's something in those boxes up front for everyone. Pass them out. Merry Christmas." As they leave, they have music playing, "What do the lonely do at Christmastime?"

So even those with bad character have hearts for they are Children of God and his spirit dwells in them. Also, they are touched by the Angel of God. So always remember the reason for the season; praise and worship God almighty with thanksgiving for his grace and mercy for all of us his children. Oh, Merry Christmas to all of you who help make his one blessed day.

God is alive and well in all of us this very day. And it's the same today, tomorrow, and every day for the rest of our lives, and there's nothing impossible for him for he makes even the hateful and evil ones enjoy and obey his will and purpose for life. So, as the world turns, remember we only got one life to live and it's not of our own doing but the Will of God almighty, and we're all God's children. These are the trials and tribulations of our daily life, for a better day is coming to All God's children.

Concrete and Steel

For so many years, I lived in a shadow. I tried hard to live a peaceful life. I cannot say normal life for I know not what that is.

I cannot escape this Dark Shadow for the concrete is hard, and the steel is cold. The dark shadow always find a way to creep upon me. I'm alone.

For so many years, I tried to hide in my corner, fighting battles and dreams inside of my mind, quietly afraid to say something.

I fear opening up to this dark side that lies inside of me. Oh, my life, how daunting it is. Madness, fail to comprehend. I am forever judged by idiocy.

For years I have hidden it as best I could. This anger will not allow me peace. Many nights I cry myself to sleep.

Sanity leaves me when the sky is purple, I ponder, "Why me? Somebody tell me why it had to be me."

Eyes of Darkness and Lonely Days

My eyes are fire filled, pure
Hell living in dark space anger flies out
Of them fiery darts of demons.

You closely it's only the Essence
Of living to tell two decades of
Isolated pain and fear Thirty Nine
Years of brown and red stalking years
Of pain.

Yet I live another day hope filled
This morning I share words of sorrow
And pain as I look out across the
Homeland and empty sky seeing no
Trees nothing moving not even a breeze.

My view is limited and downpour
Of rain is cold from the threatening
Storm the earth is cloudy with
Darkness as I scratch and scrawl
With my sanity to shape a peace
Of tranquility.

Future

My future, do I really have one?

Where does it begin, when all I know begins in the pen, 14,620 days: man that's "4" four decades.

What can I say? What can I do to begin to know what life is out there for me? Once again, where do I begin?

I've lost so much, and there's so much to see, so much to experience. So many foods to taste, so many places to go. Tell me where do I start, and where do I go?

Can I really have fun and enjoy life, or will I continually make mistakes, embarrassing myself? Will I always put my life under the gun?

Will I be too emotional and affectionate, too full of fun because I want it so abundantly with happiness and love that I keep that sense of fear always in me? One day at a time, I need help to pave my way. I'll just walk my path and live day by day.

Isaiah Shaw

211571

I am 211571 reduced to living in a cage
My heart is filled with envy and rage
Night after night I dream of better days
It's law enforcement's job to protect and serve
But what happens when they don't uphold their end
If I don't uphold mine they bring in reserve
Then do to me what they believe I deserve
Everyone's plan's to rebel but to no prevail
At times I can't trust my brothers even they would tell
I could break out and take my freedom but
I know I'd fail, in all reality I'm stuck living in hell.

STEPHEN COMBS

Where Is My Abacus?

Today is the fourth day of the month. I say this because I just discovered a behavioral pattern I often use in prison as a way to mark time. I know this sounds nebulous, so let me clear it up for you.

How a convict does his time and counts his days varies from person to person. At the beginning of my long sentence, I didn't think about marking my time. I was so overwhelmed and numb. So I just did it. Often in prison, I've heard this little maxim: "Just do the time. Don't let the time do you."

But now, as my time is getting shorter and freedom is on the horizon, I am more aware. A few days ago, I began to consider the math.

Mathematically speaking, ten (10) years is actually three-thousand six-hundred and fifty days (3,650). So twenty years would be seven-thousand three-hundred days (7,300). I have one-hundred and fifty (150) days remaining to serve. So I have served seven-thousand one-hundred and fifty (7,150) days.

During these final days, time has seemed to slow down. My psychologist explained a theory called Separation Anxiety. The fear in our minds that something will happen that will prevent the front gate from opening and us going home. Time just stops, or so it seems.

Free-world people just can't comprehend the ticking of the daily, weekly, or yearly clock. Their days go by in a blur. They're stimulated and occupied with their jobs, wife, kids, friends, and life in general. And for dormant, unstimulated convicts, their time clock goes by a tick tock at a time. But unlike most, I stay very busy. I actually try to pattern my prison days similar to one of my former free-world days.

But back to my point on what I realized about my thinking on time. I have a calendar. Actually a few of them for different functions and purposes. However, I do not have the proverbial prison calendar where each day is "X'd" out day-by-day. Or the one you see in prison movies that is "X'd" out on the concrete walls with a rock. But as I said earlier, today is the fourth day of the month. Today someone told me they needed to meet with me on the 17th. I was very excited to hear this news as I had been anticipating this meeting for months. This discussion is an integral part of my upcoming re-entry plan. In fact, a huge part of my re-entry plan depends on the information and the outcome I'll learn at this meeting.

So I grabbed my planning calendar. It's the month-at-a-glance style that I've used in my free-world office before. I noted the 17th first of all. Then I counted the days from the 4th until the 17th. That was 13 days. Periodically, I would do a countdown like I would do till Christmas Day, we'll say. It gives me a point to look forward to in the future. So instead of counting the calendar day by day, a big two-week chunk will be lobbed off of my 150-day balance. I do the same thing with sporting events, special TV events, or birthdays. Like now, I have been looking forward to the beginning of the 2020 NASCAR race season. The Daytona 500 will be held on February 16, 2020. So I've had a 30-day countdown. Every once in a while, I'll do a spot-check on the countdown. Now it's only two weeks away and counting.

Admittedly, this is a strange way to mark time. I just discovered today what I was actually doing. Anything is better than an "X" on the wall or a calendar one day at a time. What would you do to mark the time?

Prison Is

Prison is . . . sad, corrupt, depriving, cruel, vile, criminal, real, unfair, harrowing, nuts, monotonous, physically and mentally demanding, cliquish, venomous, divisive, unhealthy, oppressive, monitored, racial, vicious, deceitful, wicked, cold, hot, dank, dark, amoral, diverse, unsettling, sensory deprived, sobering, disturbing, volatile, political, the bottom of the barrel, painful, lonely, crowded, abusive, violent, unstable, unforgettable, uncaring, the ultimate time-out, a chosen destination, complicated, a learning experience, lots of unknowns, frightening, isolating, humbling, embarrassing, imminently threatening, horrible, drug-infested, menacing, gruesome, madness in a maze, full of moronic people, misgoverned, nameless, menacing, morose, a netherworld, misguided, mismanaged, noisy, monochrome, noxious, necessary, and full of bootlickers.

Maneuvering Prison Life

This is a tough subject to write about. How to move through the labyrinth that exists in prison is the most challenging issue of my life. I have decided that I should place my thoughts and observations on paper for everyone to see.

I have been working on this topic for 19 years and 8 months. I am not even close to perfecting the puzzle. Probably never will. I even thought of writing or consulting on a book: Convicting for Dummies. All of the Dummy series that I have read were very helpful. With the national prison population nearing three million, there would be a captive audience, pun intended.

One of the reasons that it's such a difficult subject is that doing time has changed and evolved so much since I began. I have also made it my mission not to become what we call being "institutionalized." I strive to keep the mindset that I'm just a resident passing through.

Let's begin with an overview of the big picture. I often read that Madagascar is the melting pot of the world. I personally think that prison is a huge melting pot. I've referred to it as a sociologist's dream. A mixture of races, ethnic diversities, gender beliefs, religions, political ideologies, education, rearing, views on criminal behavior and punishments, mental health, medical health, age, socioeconomic backgrounds, and the list goes on. Now throw all of these people in prison for 24 hours a day, 7 days a week, for years at a time, and order them to play pretty and get along. Ain't gonna happen.

When I came to prison in 1997, I tried to learn the ropes, so to speak, from the older convicts. It was different back then. One of the cardinal rules then was to never disrespect or mistreat an older convict. But the younger inmates of today don't even respect themselves, so how could they ever respect the older convicts?

Back in those beginning days, someone gave me a paper with some typed rules on it. Probably a clerk had typed it. I wish I still had the copy. I can't remember them all, but I'll try.

- If you didn't put it down, don't pick it up.
- If you didn't turn it on, don't turn it off.
- If you didn't open it, don't close it.
- If you weren't asked, then don't answer.
- Don't ask anyone about their crime or how long they have.
- Do not stare at anyone.
- Stay to yourself.
- Do not involve yourself with cliques or gangs.
- Be very careful who you associate with.
- Never go in debt.
- Do not gamble.
- Don't do the police's job for them. Let them do it themselves.
- Don't ever let your prison job let you forget who you are and where you are.

The list could be endless. But common sense and respect are major factors to consider.

Accept the fact that there are some people in prison that you will not get along with. But that is true in the free world as well. Because of the nature and design of prison, it's very difficult to completely get away from these people. In the free world, you simply retreat to your home and you are free of them. There have been many inmates that trip my internal radar. I try to avoid them if at all possible. Several times in my prison life, I've realized that I am in a conversation with a sociopath or a psychopath. Believe me, they are here. But being totally candid, I think it's much better that they are in here with me and not in the free world with my family, kids, friends, co-workers, or other citizens. But learning to circumnavigate these particular villains is a challenge at best.

Then you must deal with certain inmates that want to run or control something or someone. Always remember that no one convict is over or in charge of another convict. That is an area where I draw a line in the sand. Officers and staff, yes. But when another convict attempts to lord over me, I will politely educate him. And prison is full of these actors.

There was a big, black, 50-ish convict with me at CMCF during my first year. Did I say he was big? I was 6'6" tall and weighed around 260 lbs. He made me look tiny. We will call him Durwood. He had a speech issue, but you could understand him. Several years prior, Parchman would stage a rodeo using convicts. The governor, other dignitaries, and guests were invited. Well, Durwood would rope the bulls and steers. Word was, he got kicked in the head one day and ended up with a speech problem. So he was sent to the medical disability unit at CMCF. He was our groundskeeper. Tended to all the flower beds and scrubs. He disliked unnecessary noise and disturbances. One morning before breakfast, an argument was taking place on the zone. All of a sudden, he hopped up on one of the dayroom tables and got everyone's attention. He said, very loudly, "All y'all in here rape, rob, and kill everybody, then come to the penitentiary and wanna be the damn President of the United States. You ain't running nothing but yo mouth." Slowly, he got a standing ovation. Couldn't have said it any better myself.

Jealousy, envy, and backstabbing are extremely prevalent in the prison environment. There again, these are behaviors that you will find in the free world. The big difference is that we are constantly confined in close quarters 24/7.

All of us have lost by coming to prison, and I don't just mean our freedom. Family, homes, jobs, and some more than others. The majority never had jobs or careers. No savings or bank accounts. No 401k retirement accounts. Most inmates earned their money from illegal activities. When they were arrested, the income ceased to exist.

Then other groups of inmates have burnt, or rather, torched bridges connecting them to their family and friends. So they have nothing. No moral or financial support. No funds to purchase snacks, stamps, or personal hygiene items from the prison store. And no one to accept a collect call from. With no money or family support, they have a very bleak prison future. That will make most people very bitter. So, if human nature is any predictor, they tend to take it out on those close around them. These inmates can be difficult to maneuver around.

Now you have the ones that worked all their lives. Those that have retired, and military vets, or those with a wife, family, or girlfriends that still have bridges that are made of concrete. They can call home to family or other friends. Money can be placed on what is called an MDOC Inmate Trust Account to spend with the prison commissary. This is a good thing to be able to buy food items. The prison food leaves a lot to be desired.

This can also present issues to the inmate that makes it to the store. You are allowed to spend up to $100 per week. I never spend anywhere near that limit, but others do. The inmates that never makes purchases are always wanting or begging. This is not all of them. Some don't have any respect. Then others do, but the last group is in the minority.

Those that don't make the store often resort to their street ways. Thefts, outright robberies, and extortion schemes on the weak or older inmates are a problem. I am benevolent to others. Mama always taught me that to go forward in life, one must give back. But my rule is that it's my choice, and not because you are always asking. I don't like to see people go to bed hungry, so I share. Some I've given to will take the gift to the cigarette or dope man and trade it off. A quick way to get zeroed off my gift list. I've learned that they would take my gifts to the gambling table. Another no-no in my book. Eat it or use it and enjoy.

But who to give to and who not to is a very fine line that you must walk. Inmates can feel slighted or offended very easily. You must remain cognizant of this at all times. If you have and they don't, inmates can be very envious. This is another trait that you will find in life and the free world. But the constant togetherness of this environment makes it more problematic. Inmates will retaliate with vicious rumors and outright lies to staff or other inmates if they feel you have somehow wronged them. This is true, whether real or imagined. And in their mind, not sharing what is essentially yours gives them just cause. Sad, but true. Fights even break out if they push the issue. There are more fights on Commissary Day than any other day. Usually it's a debt collection issue or someone wants what's not theirs. Stay away from debts and make good choices if you show charity.

I've also found that inmates can feel threatened by people they perceive as educated. It appears if they feel you are smarter than they are, you are somehow better than they are. These inmates feel very intimidated. I've discovered by working for the education department that the average education level in the MDOC is 5th grade. You must learn not to talk over their heads. I try to be helpful when asked, but I never volunteer information or advice. Then only cautiously.

Over the years, I've had many inmates bring me letters from family, loved ones, and friends. Also, legal letters from attorneys and the courts. They would ask me to read them out loud. I would gladly do so. Then they would ask me to write them back. I did, but I had a rule. The first three letters read and replied to were for free. Any more letters and they would be required to sign up for the ABE/GED classes and the reading class. I tutored the reading class at EMCF Meridian. I had a thought one day that I proposed to the EMCF Education Director. The idea was to start a primer book reading program. The idea was approved by the Warden and the Corporate Education Director. Several books were purchased and off we went. I am proud to say that six students learned to read over the time I was there. They could not read an "or," "a," "and," "but," "cat," or "dog" before they began. Good memories. Inmates seemed to accept tutors because they saw the help you were offering.

But negotiating the slippery path of your education and knowledge with other inmates can be a tricky path. I learn something new every day of my life. I learn from other inmates. But learning to balance is the key for me. Some inmates feel slighted and get their feelings hurt. Most of the time, you are totally unaware. I think it must be a lack of self-confidence or a self-esteem issue. Learning to maneuver this prison matter is akin to traversing a mine field.

Next is inmate/staff relations. Never fraternize with staff, especially female. Or male, if you are gay. That is a train wreck in the offing. Plus, an inmate should never spend a lot of time with an officer. Other inmates will think that you are snitching on them. My early training on how to act in prison taught me to never get closer than an arm's length to a staff member. There are exceptions, such as when I worked as an administrative clerk or a tutor. Then you had to interact with staff, sometimes in an office setting. The best advice is to address the staff as Officer, Sir, Ma'am, or Mr. and Mrs./Ms. And always say, yes, ma'am or no ma'am, and yes, sir or no sir. Don't forget: please, thank you, and excuse or pardon me. Basic etiquette. Be polite and professional. I will admit that I have had to bite my tongue many times over the years. Biting of the tongue is a much better alternative to choose. Any staff member can give you a written disciplinary infraction report (RVR) for breaking the rules. Knock on wood, but I have never had an RVR in 19 years and 8 months.

I cannot sit here and claim to know all the right and wrong things there are about how to get along in prison. And I hope I never do. This is such a different world but one that I am a part of. It's a world without rhyme and reason. Prison marches to its own unique beat unlike any I've known. Some inmates are so institutionalized by being locked up 30 and 40 years plus. One guy here with me today just completed his 49th year. Enough is enough, I say. Their hearts have become as hard as steel. But the 49-year guy has God in his life. He is always calm and peaceful. I don't know how he does it. Many suffer from arrested development due to the fact that they were incarcerated at such tender ages. No social, mental, or educational growth whatsoever. More obstacles to maneuver.

I talked to a 40-year old guy once. He was really into handguns. I asked him if he ever carried a gun? And he said, "Like all my life." So I then asked when, at what age did he start carrying? He replied, "When I was 11." I'm thinking, What! Eleven! Wow! When I was eleven, I had marbles, jack rocks, bubble gum, and maybe a baby frog to scare a girl with. But not a handgun, for God's sake. He asked me if I ever carried a pistol. And I said, "Yes, a Colt .45 when I was in the U.S. Army." He told me that everyone in his town carried a pistol. I'm thinking Gun Smoke or the Wild Wild West. But this is the diversity that we live with in prison. I cannot fathom living in a town where eleven-year-old kids feel like they must carry a gun.

I know that I have just touched the tip of the iceberg about how to act in prison. What to do and what not to do as a prisoner. But maneuvering life in prison has been the most difficult task for me to master. As I stated previously, I am not institutionalized but just a resident passing through.

How to walk through the maze of life while in prison is a question much bigger than I am. I hope I have shed some light on this subject and given you thoughts to ponder. The memories held within this story are things that will stay with me forever.

Kindness

Many moons ago I began this prison journey. Back in 1997, I was sent to CMCF in Rankin County from Jackson County. My first stop on that long grip was at a Hardee's Restaurant. You heard right . . . a Hardee's. It was a small town on Hwy 49 called Magee. It happened because of the kindness of one of the transportation deputies from the Jackson County sheriff's office. A large number of jail inmates were being sent that day. More than seventy of us just from Jackson County. Back in 1997, there was a big issue between county sheriff's and MDOC. MDOC was overcrowded and so were the county jails. Inmates that had been sentenced were staying excessive amounts of time in the county jails. Some of them staying from eight months to over a year.

So that day the bus was full. Two of us were left over as the bus was at capacity. I was one of the two, along with a trustee who was the cook at the jail. The sheriff decided to let us ride separately in a Ford Crown Vic patrol car. Our driver was Deputy Harold. He was one of the county bailiffs and a nice officer. Nearly 79 and near retirement, he was easy going. I was in front with him, and Jimmy the cook was in back. We were following the bus up Hwy 49 when, all of a sudden, he pulled off at Hardee's in Magee.

He told us he had been making this trip to Rankin and Parchman for many, many years and he always stopped for breakfast. Jimmy and I were shocked, especially when he pulled up to the ordering mic and gave the girl his instructions. He ordered his usual bacon, egg, and cheese with a large coffee. Then he ordered us a Hardee's Big Breakfast, with hash browns, gravy and biscuits, pancakes, and a large coffee each. We had eggs, grits, and a jelly biscuit plus all the sides he ordered. He said we might as well have a good meal before we get to MDOC. The ironic thing is that the date was July 17, 1997, which happens to have been my birthday. YES, I came to prison for my first time at age 45.

Years later I heard through the grapevine that Deputy Harold had passed away. He was a kind man and one that brought smiles to two convicts' faces on the infamous day.

Humbled

Prison is humiliating and humbling.
We are stripped bare of dignity and assets.
We have nothing left.
Cast into hell we look upward for a way out.

Dick Biscuits

I've named these personally seasoned specialty prison food items Dick Biscuits or Dick Cornbread.

For years, while in prison, I have observed a host of men that have created these so-named delicacies.

I feel that good hygiene is a taught skill. I thank my parents for instilling the routine of good hand washing into my brain.

However, daily I see my fellow prisoners hop outta bed for breakfast and head to the bathroom to take their morning piss. Then they head directly to the chow hall by bypassing the ALL important sink with the soap and running water.

Sometimes I mumble, and other times I say it aloud, "Enjoy your Dick Biscuits."

The very hand they used to point and stream with is the same hand that will soon hold that hot and delicious morning biscuit. That's why I call them "Dick Biscuits."

That same process is repeated at lunch and dinner, except then I call it "Dick Cornbread."

Some guys will stop at the sink just long enough to turn on the faucet, stick the fingers of one hand under the water for a heartbeat or two, and then head off for their "Dick Biscuit."

I'm not certain if they actually dip the offending hand (fingers) under the water because I don't observe that closely.

But whether you hold your Johnson with your right or left hand, you are adding personal flavor and lots of nasty to your diet.

But to the credit of many, we do wash our hands faithfully and not just after trips to the urinal. Frequency is the key.

A pause of only twenty seconds, with soap and water, and your biscuit or cornbread can be hot and delicious, and also Dick-free.

Here's to your Health.

Bon Appetit.

Prison Journal

Christmas Day 12/25/19

Today I completed 7,108 days of prison time. Less than 200 to go. I thought we had a good meal today. Ham, turkey, green beans, mashed potatoes, dressing with gravy, roll, and cake. No cranberry sauce. But I was thankful. Lot of guys bitched but tend to bitch as a rule. We had chocolate milk at breakfast. A treat.

Over two months with no yard call. The weather was warm today. Above normal readings. My elusive pecan tree is still looming in my window. I'm afraid the pecans are just rotting on the ground. Short on staff.

12/26/19

I'm concerned about my friend, Richard. He had pneumonia at Thanksgiving and was hospitalized at the Parchman hospital. He was discharged about a week ago. He's 68 years old, and this episode really took the wind out of his sails. His strength and memory are zapped. I'm helping him as I know he would help me.

Christmas Day Update 12/25/19

We have a new guy, Mr. Bell, that I hope will join our class. He told me that he's getting a new TV in a few days. He asked if I could help him find a TV stand. MDOC provides us with a stand made at the metal/iron fabrication shop here at Parchman. There are a limited amount, and none were available. They are nifty little designed deals that hook over our iron bed rails. I'm not a mechanic, but I love engineering a project. So I located an old unused walker, some cardboard, medical paper tape, and an old bedsheet. Several years ago, I made an exact scale 7-foot-long cloth measuring tape. It's accurate from 1 foot, 1 inch, ½, ¼, and ⅛ inch. It's come in very handy more than once. So, I measured the area, width, and depth of the space on top of the walker where a tabletop would sit. Then I cut the cardboard and sandwiched three pieces together. Then, I taped the three together and made a sturdy triangular table top. I then centered the top and secured the top to the walker using long strips of the old sheet. I folded the remaining sheet and covered the cardboard designed tabletop. A lower accessory shelf, 26" x 11", was formed the same way and secured. A bath towel was placed over it, and he was amazed and pleased. I was also happy.

In prison we call that "convicting," making something from nothing or learning to work with what we've got and surviving.

December 28, 2019

Not all discoveries are good. Take my discovery today, for example. While figuring out the exact number of days that I must complete in 2020 till I can go home, leap year reared its lonesome head. I had originally calculated 28 days for the month of February, until I looked at my new 2020 calendar. And, yes, 2020 is a leap year with 29 days. So MDOC gets one extra day before I can depart.

12/30/19 Monday

Last night we were placed on state-wide lockdown. It continues today. No dayroom, no outside fresh air, and no visits to my elusive pecan tree. All meals are brought to our rooms in Styrofoam trays. I attend physical therapy sessions and was surprised that MDOC allowed our therapist to have our workout. He said Unit 31 was the only one allowed to have our sessions at Parchman. The therapy is very helpful to me. I am in a wheelchair due to a balance issue, and I'm working hard to free myself of the dreaded chair. Not sure how long the lockdown will last. We are hearing that it's due to gang-related activity at one of the other state facilities.

12/31/19 Tuesday New Year's Eve

Still on lockdown. The officer is keeping us in our rooms and out of the hall. We can go to and from the bathroom and the microwave. The problem is that the rooms are like meat lockers. We do not have heat in our rooms or in our building, for that matter. I have been in the same room for two years without heat. On the nights it gets into the teens, twenties, and thirties, it's way too cold. The staff reports the issue, but no solution as of yet. This is a medical disability unit. Parchman maintenance guys come over periodically and attempt a fix, but to no avail.

12/31/19

Tate sucks got my attention tonight. I just learned that MDOC Commissioner Pelicia Hall just resigned. Also Marshal Fisher. Sounds like Tate Sucks is cleaning house for 2020.

12/31/19 Tuesday night New Year's Eve

As I lie here on my bed at Unit 31 in Parchman, I'm watching the live TV coverage at New York's Time Square. A million people celebrating the coming of the new year. Over 20,000 city, state, and federal law enforcement officers armed to the hilt. Uniformed, plain clothes, aviation units, snipers on the roofs, and ultra-high-tech drones keeping the revelers safe and secure.

And here I am in the state's infamous Delta penitentiary. Now, I'm surrounded by murderers, rapists, bank robbers, train robbers, and a cattle rustler or two. But I feel safer in this bed than at Times Square. That is a bull's eye for every whack-a-doodle in the world. Understand that I said, this bed, at this unit. Some units here at Parchman are not so safe.

01/01/20 Wednesday New Year' Day 6:00 am

Just saw the local news. A 40-year-old inmate was stabbed to death at SMCI in Greene County. And MDOC Commissioner Hall's and Marshall Fisher's resignations and retirement are official.

01/02/20 Thursday morning at about 7:30 AM

A gang riot broke out last night at Unit 29 here at Parchman. That is a lockdown unit. Twenty-one hospitalized, and the Sunflower County coroner reporting one inmate found stabbed to death in his cell. The Parchman farm is abuzz with first responders and Mississippi

Highway Patrol. I, on the other hand, am thankful to be where I am, which is Unit 31.

01/02/20 Thursday around 3:00 PM
About seven ambulances and a small fleet of MS Highway Patrol cars just blew past our building here at Parchman. The word from Inmate.com is that the violence (gang) has spread to Unit 30A Building.

01/02/20 Thursday around 6:00 PM
Local TV described a riot at Unit 30 A and B building. One found dead in his cell with many more injured. Since Unit 31 houses the Parchman firefighters, they were dispatched to Unit 30. The fire was put out, and the men returned to the building. Tension is high, but 31 is calm.

01/03/2020 Friday morning around 10:00 AM
Local TV reported another inmate killing at Chickasaw County Regional Facility. A young white male inmate and several others injured in what they described as a riot. Where will it end?

Services are being affected here at Parchman. The breakfast food truck just arrived about four hours late. Our laundry was not picked up last night. No canteen or visitation. Staff is getting edgy and short. Just laying low and to myself. I want to be able to wear the t-shirt "I survived the 2020 riots at Parchman."

01/03/2020 Friday morning around 11:00 AM
Unconfirmed reports that yet another inmate was killed at Unit 29 around 2 AM to 3 AM. Also reports that 400 inmates were moved back to Unit 32. Unit 32 was closed down and shuttered up several years ago. I remember it being condemned. Word is, they swept it out, turned on the cold water, and locked them in. Now I'm concerned about violence on staff.

01/03/2020 Friday evening around 5:00 PM
Local TV news confirms another inmate killed at Unit 29 in Parchman. Also according to Sunflower County Sheriff James Haywood, MDOC

did reopen Unit 32. It has been closed for eight years. No heat or hot water.

01/04/2020 Saturday morning around 9:00 AM
Today is the birthday of my ex-wife and the mother of my only daughter. Hey, Faye, I'm thinking about you.

Also, more Parchman drama. It is reported that two inmates have escaped from Parchman. In the middle of all the chaos. I predict Superintendent Marshal Turner's days are numbered.

Also, my 2020 predictions. Buy Apple, Microsoft, McDonald's, Visa, and GEO private prison stock.

And now Inmate.com has the escapees up to three.

01/04/2020 Saturday night around 6:30 PM
We do have three inmates on the run. My PTSD has been tweaked up a notch or two. Just outside Unit 31's fence is the Parchman Fire Department and CID Headquarters. MS Highway Patrol cars, four ambulances, and rows of other law enforcement lined our front. Also a helicopter sits at the ready. They are staging for something. Just shows you how real this is.

01/05/2020 Sunday morning around 10:30 AM
All is quiet. The chopper is gone. Reinforcements are still on the farm but not in front of Unit 31. Our class is scheduled for tomorrow, but I'm not sure if they will allow the professor. The LSU championship game is only eight days away.

I read some disturbing and very disappointing news last night. US District Judge Barbour finally ruled on the much-anticipated case against MDOC regarding the operation of the private mental health prison at Meridian. He ruled for MDOC and against the Southern Poverty Law Center and the ACLU.

It was a class action suit that began in 2013 and ended in a six-week trial in March/April 2018. I was a named plaintiff as well as a testifying plaintiff. It was about rampant gang violence with deaths and stabbings, food, lack of mental and medical care, long-term segregation, staff corruption, short staffing, drugs, and gangs actually running the prisons. Compelling testimony from many expert witnesses was given. However, Judge Barbour ruled for MDOC. I won't be able to call the SPLC or ACLU attorneys until Monday, but I'm sure that an appeal will be filed. The Alabama prison system was also sued at around the same time for very similar issues. The trials were only months apart. But the federal judge there ruled very shortly after their trial. He ordered sweeping and landmark changes to the Alabama prisons. The same was expected in Mississippi. And the beat goes on.

01/05/2020 Sunday

One of the escaped prisoners was caught, and one remains missing. They supposedly left on two 4-wheelers and drove to Shelby, where they stole a 2011 GMC pickup truck.

Reports are that MS Highway Patrol are manning two thirty-five person teams for two shifts each to guard the inmates at Units 29 and 32.

Very little running water is at Unit 32.

Many cell doors won't lock, so a constant presence is needed.

01/06/2020 Monday morning around 8:15 AM

Local TV showed several photos of the living conditions at Parchman. They were taken by the MS Department of Health during an inspection in June 2019. The report talked about the food, mold, water, no lights, heat, and lack of bedding.

The report went on to say that US Congressman Bennie Thompson has asked that the US Attorney General investigate the living, food, safety, staffing, and environmental conditions at Parchman. He said that what is occurring is unacceptable.

01/06/2020 Monday evening around 5:15 PM

Local news reported that escapee #2 was recaptured in Tennessee.

01/07/2020 Tuesday morning around 9:30 AM

Reports are that the situation is bleak for the guys at Unit 32. No running water; they are bringing them bottled water. Stripped naked, put into their cells, no mats, no bedding. All personal property thrown away. No TVs, no radios, nothing. State troopers are in charge.

01/07/2020

About fifteen state troopers just came through Unit 31. Six or seven of them came through our room. Very nice and polite. Talked for about two minutes, then left. We were expecting a shake down, but nothing yet. The two troopers that came to my bedside seemed genuinely concerned that we were OK.

They were dressed in full battle mode. Their bulletproof vests were emblazoned with the letters SOG. I asked him if it stood for Special Operations Group, and he smiled and said, "Yes." He then asked if I was military, and I said, "Yes, Army." The trooper then said, "We're gonna keep you safe; don't worry." I guess he could sense the concern. We were prepared for the worst like when K-9 comes blazing in, but their visit actually had the opposite effect. It was calming.

01/08/2020 Wednesday morning around 11:00 AM

Reports coming in are disturbing. An inmate threw piss in the face of Superintendent Turner as he was walking around Unit 32. As expected, the inmate was beaten severely.

I also learned that they have around 550 inmates at Unit 32. They were placed in there with no clothes, no bedding, no mats. There is no running water. They are given bottled water.

The most senseless discovery I've made concerns the inmates' property. Seems as if they moved the inmates from Unit 29 F zone to the gym at 29. However, all their personal property was packed up and taken to what is called "the Pit" at Parchman and burned. Everything. Canteens, books, photos, TVs, radios, canteen tennis shoes, obituaries, letters, legal work, and clothing.

Also, several busloads of red and white C custody inmates are being mass moved to the facility in Tutwiler, Mississippi.

All facilities state-wide are now off lockdown, except the state-run facilities.

A 100-man team of specially trained officers from Angola in Louisiana is now here to provide operational support. Also, a 100-man team from the Tennessee Department of Corrections is here.

And still no pecans.

01/09/2020 Thursday morning around 10:15 AM

Local TV did not have any Parchman news last night or this morning. Heavily escorted prisoner buses and vans are still leaving yesterday and this morning. They are surrounded by Mississippi Highway Patrol and a helicopter. Operational air support is being provided by the Mississippi Highway Patrol.

It was cold in here again last night. Still no heat. We haven't been outside for fresh air and sunshine for about three months now. My body could use a jolt of both right about now.

01/10/2020 Friday night around 10:00 PM

Strong storms coming through. Heavy thunder, lightning, and roaring winds. Sounds like a tornado. Cold in here.

01/11/2020 Saturday morning maybe 6 to 7 AM

Very dark and cold in here. The power is off. We have an emergency generator, but it's not on. It's located just outside the back door, and we can hear it from our room. It must be out of diesel fuel. That's normal. It's supposed to fire up automatically. Just another maintenance lapse in preparation. It's beginning to get light outside.

01/11/2020 Saturday morning around 10:00 AM

The maintenance truck just arrived with fuel. It should be running shortly.

It's on now. Lights are on. Only a limited amount of circuits are powered. Our three portable heaters are not working. The breakfast truck just arrived.

01/11/2020 Saturday morning around 11:00 PM

The word is that we did have a tornado or severe straight-line winds. A portion of the roof from the Spiritual Life Center is lying in the field on the side of this building. (Opposite side.) Also, a large solar panel is there as well.

Reports that between 50–75 power poles are down over the region. Clarksdale, Cleveland, Greenville, Ruleville, Drew, and, of course, Parchman are without power.

We also have no running water, as the water pump operates on electricity. I have stockpiled water in anticipation of emergencies.

01/11/2020 Saturday afternoon around 1:00 PM

Back in the dark again. The maintenance guy must have only brought a few gallons of diesel fuel. That bought us three hours.

It's a weird feeling. It's dark, dank, cold, and eerily very quiet. Nothing running, no sounds, everyone staying by their beds.

But my bedmate to my left and I are set up for this occurrence. Every wall in these rooms has a red-plate wall socket. This was a hospital, so the red sockets are e-circuits wired into the emergency generator. The socket is behind my bed. We have an eight-foot extension cord. He and I can plug in our TV, fans, etc. to the extension cord and connect to the generator when it powers up again. They moved our microwave from its usual spot to another location that has a red E-socket.

01/11/2020 Saturday afternoon around 2:30 PM

The maintenance cavalry just arrived with more fuel. We are now up and running again. Our TVs are working, and there is a beehive of activity at the community microwave. Some have stashed water; some are reheating stale coffee from breakfast. Others are attacking the ice chest to melt it in the microwave for beverages or Ramen noodles. Survival.

01/11/2020 Saturday evening around 6:00 PM

Generator is down again. Very dark and colder. I'm just wrapped up in my blanket with clothes and socks on. I don't like this feeling. I suffer from Anxiety Disorder. Being in a dark, locked building with bank robbers, train robbers, and cattle thieves, with no lights or heat, is not comforting.

01/11/2020 Saturday night around 7:30 PM
Generator is up again. Food truck just came. Cold meat sandwiches, cookies, and pineapples. I'm watching the football game wrapped up. The lights give me security and comfort.

01/11/2020 Saturday night at 10:15 PM
Gonna try to sleep.

01/12/2020 Sunday night. Middle of the night or very early morning
So cold. Down to 31 degrees. So dark I can't even see my own hands. Generator is off again; must have gone off shortly after I fell asleep. No movement in the halls.

01/12/2020 Sunday morning at 6:48 AM
I know the time, as the generator just kicked on again and my TV popped on.

I just went up front to check my morning blood sugar reading. The guard said power would probably be down for a few days. I asked if the folks had planned to bring us bottled water, as we have none to drink. She said they were supposed to have brought bottles yesterday. She also said she would call and check.

Some of the guys said the last time this happened, they brought each man eight bottles each per day. My Boy Scout, "Be Prepared," may have bought me a couple of days.

01/12/2020 Sunday morning at 10:15 AM
Generator still purring along. Still no food truck for breakfast or water delivery. And as I write this, the food truck pulls in.

01/12/2020 Sunday afternoon around 12:45 PM
Our breakfast today consisted of two slices of white bread, a 1-oz. package of peanut butter, some Bran Flakes, and some canned pineapple. No milk for the cereal or water.

I have perfected washing my hands with ice. Take three ice cubes and rub them in my hands till they melt. Then use my soap bar to wash my hands with. Then use three more ice cubes to melt, and that's the rinse. Towel dry, and I'm good to go.

Nap time.

01/12/2020 Sunday evening around 4:30

Generator is still running. We had four bottles of water delivered. The water is back on. Maintenance hooked up a generator at the water pump site. Toilets, handwashing, and showers again. Now we await the power to be restored and the lockdown to be lifted.

We will probably no doubt go dark again tonight, as the fuel will run out.

01/12/2020 Sunday night at 7:26 PM

Power was restored Yay! Yay!

01/12/2020 Sunday night at 8:15 PM

The power was short-lived. It's off again, and generator is purring.

01/13/2020 Monday afternoon around 1:00 PM

Quiet day. Disappointed that we can't watch LSU vs Clemson game. Our Direct TV Dish took a hit in the storm. Can't get ESPN.

01/13/2020 Monday night around 7:30 PM

This reminds me of living in the king's day with a town crier of the 1940s with radios and no TVs. We've got a guy in the hallway listening to the National Championship game via radio and calling out highlights and play-by-plays. Almost like being there. Go LSU Tigers!

LSU 42 – Clemson 25

01/14/2020 Tuesday morning before dawn

Bad storm again. Thunder and lightning. A flicker of the lights, and that old familiar smell of diesel fuel permeates the air. The power is down again.

01/14/2020 Tuesday morning after sunrise around 6:45 AM

The power is back on now.

01/14/2020 Tuesday morning around 10:30 AM
Tate sucks should be holding up his right hand with his left hand on the Bible.

Long live Tate sucks.

01/14/2020 Tuesday morning around 11:00 AM
Yuri, our physical therapist, shows up for our weekly workout session.

We learned from him that the Governor-elect showed up very unexpectedly at Parchman on Saturday. He went to Units 32, 29, 30, 42, hospital, and where our food is cooked. No advance warning. Best kind of inspection to have. Maybe he learned something for himself.

Trevor Hoskins

Poverty in My Childhood

During the mid '80s, I was five years old, old enough to know what the true definition of Poverty meant, because we were living it. Living in a three-bedroom house with my parents, along with eight of us, a total of ten heads in one small house, cluttered and overcrowded. I remember wearing my shoes down to the sole. My dad was the only provider, "The head of the household," with income coming in. There were so many of us my dad had to buy our shoes two pair at a time every Friday when he got paid, after all the bills were paid, from oldest to youngest. But by me being the third to the youngest who didn't take care of my shoes and clothes properly, I was at the bottom of the list for anything new. I was in the first grade when my experience of poverty occurred, when my shoe sole literally fell off of my left shoe. The shoes were made out of very low-grade material, brown with a rubber thin sole and big buckle strap on them. The kids at my school would talk about me every day. At the time, I didn't know that "sticks and stones would break my bones but words would never hurt me." I was teased so bad that one morning I took it upon myself to hide my left shoe, thinking that my parents would have sympathy for me and let me stay at home or get me another pair of shoes, but we were so poor that that didn't work. I was basically trying to get a new pair of shoes before it was my turn to get a pair. Instead, I got a beating for hiding my shoes and my mother still sent me to school with one shoe on. I cried on the bus all the way to school, looking out of the bus window hoping that the bus would catch a flat or break down before I made it to school. Once I made it to school and made it to my classroom, with red eyes, tears, and mucus running down my face, my teacher asked, what's wrong with you? I was so humiliated that I couldn't respond, I was trying to explain, but my words were broken up so much that I couldn't make a complete sentence to inform my teacher what was wrong with me. My ego and my pride were on the floor; my ego and my pride were so heavy that I needed a hundred men to help me pick them back up. My teacher pulled me out of the classroom and gave me a long ceremony about how tough times are and that everything is going to be all right. My teacher responded softly and finally got me to calm down, but I couldn't sit in class with one shoe on, because I was humiliated and tortured every day from the students about those big buckled strap shoes. After that, my teacher showed great concern. She got my address and came to my house and brought me a pair of gym shoes, I felt like I was somebody again, and my ego and my pride were uplifted for that Spirit of the Moment. I became a straight-A student with S's up and down my progress report. That was my first stage of Poverty, in my childhood.

Larry Singleton

The Gentleman's Resort of Sunflower County

Having been assigned the task of elaborating on my summer vacation and this period of time having so many enthralled, astute occurrences, I chose only a small segment of this formidable enthusiastic summer to entice your envy.

I have titled this report "The Gentleman's Resort of Sunflower County-Parchman," which I attended. In retrospect, I submit and acknowledge that this resort is only for a very select few vivacious, insolent individuals! Plainly speaking, after application, not everybody is invited to attend this resort. To qualify and be able to board the courtesy passenger van that transits throughout Mississippi, you must first be approved by an individual selected by voters in your specific county. That person and only that person can assure you a reservation. That person negotiates the length of time you are permitted to spend at this exclusive resort. After all approvals for your stay, you arrive, unload from the bus, and go to the check-in desk to be processed, where you receive your housing assignment and the clothing you are to wear.

Please notice that all guests wear either one of three colored pants: red, black, or green. This is to insure that regardless of financial worth, everyone attending this resort is on equal footing. You may be housed with a millionaire or a pauper. Every guest is treated equally by the employees.

The resort housing is comprised of multiple sized and varied designed buildings.

This resort, along with two other locations, one in central Mississippi and the other in the Southern part of the state, are owned by the Men's Diabolical Oaf's Club, Inc., commonly called MDOC.

Now some generalities about Parchman Resort. While here, you learn the intricate and special features and become familiar with these specialties to make your stay more enjoyable.

There are employees everywhere. All are there and assigned to assist you in and for your impertinent and ostentatious idiosyncrasies. As an example of their abilities and halcyon character, they are at your pleasure to debate, wrestle, box—without or with gloves—at any time and any place. Those are a few of the many sports for your choosing.

For those guests who desire knowledge of trades, such as carpentry, plumbing, painting, HVAC (air conditioning), plant taxonomy, agriculture, metal craft, clothing manufacturing, and cattle care, all those trades are taught by hands-on experience.

As you have probably noticed, this company does not provide a menu for meals. Like many other surprises here, the cuisine is also a surprise. The uniqueness of the entrees are the specialties of our chefs. One of our chefs specialty happens to be pasta, fixed 101 ways, the other chef's specialty is potatoes, fixed 101 ways. All fixed with meats, sauces, and gravies. These specialties are accompanied by side dishes of boiled, tasteless cabbage, turnip greens, and other culinary specialties. The employees are not permitted to partake of guests' foods; they are relegated to their sandwiches and chips or Vienna sausages and crackers.

So, if you find yourself desiring something different, then make application to visit by participating in one of the events described in the resort's brochure that will guarantee you a visit to our Parchman Gentleman's Resort.

In the event you ask, when you see all the buildings with 10-feet-high chain-link fence, with razor wire atop the fences, the reason is to keep outsiders out! They want to bring mobile phones with them to take pictures of the unique resort. They are not allowed.

Come and visit. You will probably not like everything, but the Mississippi Department of Corrections is terribly unique. Well, you probably won't like anything at the prison at Parchman, Mississippi.

How was your summer? This was mine!

Prison Poem 1

When I entered the Mississippi legal system
On the wrong side of the law, but not guilty,
I was totally unaware of the pitfalls,
And the lack of competency and truthfulness of its members.

I only knew how a trial was conducted,
By the rules I saw on TV—Perry Mason.
On TV good always prevails and bad goes away.
From the good cop, bad cop, and lying investigators,

To the unjust and wayward judges in the black,
That are supposed to keep justice true and fair,
Most are biased, prejudiced, and show predetermination.
The court appointed attorneys are even worse.

Plead them, then more cases, more money.
Truth and fairness be damned! Next case!
After the gavel falls, last one to the bar for drinks,
Is a sloppy squire!

Prison Poem 2

OK, big boy, you're at the big house now, move.
When you go anywhere, with more than one—walk in a line!
Shut up and don't talk, eyes straight forward.
That's the second thing I heard when I arrived here!
That was at A & C in Rankin County.
I was scared to death until I noticed that
No one else paid any attention to the big fat gruffy
Black officer that sat on a stool when issuing orders,
Because his fat stomach hindered his breathing.
I answered the doctor's 1001 questions.
Then the psych dr. What's today? Who's president? Then finally
He says, Do you hear voices especially at night? Yes!
"Yes?" He looks at me, a smile, as if to say, this one's mine.
I clarified, "Only when my wife was alive!"
His demeanor changes. He frowns, "Get the hell out of here!"
After time passes, I realize many of the guards
Must have a GED diploma for school because
They only use a vocabulary of less than 25 words other
Than the traditional 6: bastard, bitch, S.O.B., G.D., M.F.
And just plain fuck!
If I could only have a breath of fresh air with
Intelligent words, it would be as refreshing
As mountain clean, clean, crisp fresh air!
These Einsteins of the vocabulary are so proficient
That they cannot decide how to unscrew the tooth paste cap.
So after brushing they leave the cap lying!

Prison Poem 3

Now about prison life in general.
Mail call—when the officer gets off her lazy keester!
Sick call—turn in the request, wait 8-10 days, only if you are alive!
Food—no seasoning. All soybeans taste the same!
Ri??Riter—promises you the moon, delivers dirt!
S.O.P.—Standard Operating Procedure—only to protect MDOC!
New Friend—an inmate that sees you as sheep to be sheared!
Guard—an ex-sanitation employee with a uniform!
Doctor—a person serving sentence because of too many prescriptions!
Church—a meeting place to deliver drugs to fellow inmates!
Ole School—inmate over 50!
Pops—inmate over 70!
Case Manager—supposed to know how, but not when!
Warden—officer that knows how to duck problems and survive!
Commissioner—head knocker can't find an answer, sol???e!
You're welcome for my clarification of positions.

Prison Poem 4

Now we look forward to the future.
For some 10 years, 20 years, or no hope!
The past is history, not to be remembered!
Though they be very few, bright spots are to remember,
Quaint individuals to glue to the Gray,
And 1% guards that exhibit compassion, or brains!
When we leave we WILL never forget
A friend that helped me through—
A warden that spoke encouragement.
I hope to see them on the outside!
But will it be 10 years, 20 years, or no hope?

A Poem Is a Tree

A poem is like a tree.
It has many branches like the oak, pine, and sycamore.
The tree has many inhabitants like birds, bugs, all free/
They grow to many shapes and sizes, even more
Like the sequoia, too massive, so strong, it could build a house
For a human, bird, beetle, or a mouse.
The limbs have many directions, right, left, up or down.
So does my poem, from rhyme to plane in only one line,
But I notice as I read "Dream Cabinet," there's not uniformity
To give iambic pentameter or any other meter.
So I am cleared for today and a poem remains like a tree,
Tall, non-directional except up, up to the tall sky with no meter.

Parchman Diary

12-21-19 - Saturday

Today is Saturday. I am still remembering just how delicious the food was that the professor brought. As I read in my narrative, I read for the class, despite being in prison at Parchman, "It's beginning to feel a lot like Christmas for me, especially since I can now begin to look forward to possibly spending the next Christmas at my home I own, in North Mississippi. I have already been thinking what I'll do for that Christmas for my family of two sons, four grandsons, four granddaughters, one daughter in law, and six great-grandchildren. Since I have missed a large volume of past Christmases, the next one will be a very special one. The Family, "Ain't seen nothin' like it!" I will make it a "thing to remember!"

We had a decent breakfast, lunch, and dinner. It was eatable.

I sat in my wheelchair next to my window and watched the birds after I fed them. They are just like humans. Get four or five eating on a piece of bread and one decides to run off with the glob of bread leaving the remainder to find another piece of bread.

I have this date started reworking even further a short story I plan to send to a magazine publisher to see if they will purchase it. Hopefully they will, so I can break into the industry with a published short story. Tomorrow is Sunday so it remains to be seen what will transpire.

A funny thing happened today. An inmate here that was acting crazy or mental problems and loud and pretentious, as his usual self, started early before sun rise. He was boisterous and violent, swinging at people with his fist. This type of behavior is getting worse, day by day. Other inmates complained to security. Apparently today broke the straw and he was told to pack up he was being moved to 42 (the hospital). He said and kept stating emphatically, "I ain't going to 42. You cannot make me!" He repeated this frequently.

K-9 arrived to [carry] him. He left his room doing everything he could do to stop his wheelchair from being pushed up front to go to the van. All the way to the front he kept repeating, "I am not going to 42!" When he arrived up front and saw one officer, he repeated "I'm not going." Three other K-9 came up to him and told him he was going. He said "Oh Lord, I'm surrounded!" Then he capitulates and said, "Let's go!" We had a good laugh. It surely was quiet the rest of the day!

12-22-19 – Sunday

No church today! And that's tragic. I keep a running battle with these hierarchy that are supposed to promote an idea, and knowledge, that a spiritual experience with a higher power can present a very definite change in an individual's character and outlook on the future. It can change a person's total relationship with friends, family, neighbors, and even enemies. I have witnessed very definite changes in the overall character of an individual.

Permit me to digress and relay an experience at 720 [CMET] with a young gang member.

We first met, me a 74 year old and him a 26 year old, at the microwave. "Ole man," he said, "get the hell out of my way or I will whep your ass." He was very belligerent and mad at the world. I moved back and let him use the microwave, but it was obvious I was not completed. He finished and left. There was something about this young man that caught my attention and it was not a "perverted thought." "He needs God in his life!" I started simply saying, "Good morning, Juan," when we met. That was all. Even this greeting seemed to irritate him. One morning he said quit greeting me. I kept on. After a period of about two or three months he came to my rack with a very definite intention of "having it out with me!" We talked, I was always calm and collected and he agitated and ready to go to "fist city!" Finally when he apparently realized he could not elevate me to his same state of mind, he looked me directly in the eyes for a few seconds, with a changed tone of voice and grandeur and softly said "What's with you?" He hesitated.

"I mean you are so at peace with everybody. What do you have that I don't have?" Again he hesitated, awaiting an answer. I responded "God." Another long few seconds then he said, "Can this God of yours give me the peace you present and have?" I said, "Sure." I saw at that time a young man waiting, waiting for a chance for peace. I very easily without condemning his past actions told him about God and how he could have my peace—God's peace. He accepted.

A very definite and explicit change began to evolve in Juan. After then frequently Juan would sit with me and we would talk.

After another couple of months Juan was moved to another building, but many times as we zones transited to the Dining Hall I would hear a jovial voice yell out. "Good morning, Mr. Larry!" I would look and of course it was Juan.

Now my point to this story is, these so-called religious leaders the chaplains and building "religious advisors" appear to me to have only a title, but take no responsibility for their title. I am sure they cover their posterior with questionable reports because the religious advisor for our building told me one time he had to make a report of anything under his authority. A one-line report would cover all he had to actually report.

When I volunteered to institute and follow thru on a Sunday worship service, rather amazingly on the next calendar of monthly events a 9 a.m. Sunday morning worship service was scheduled. That raises a question in my mind of how visitation on Sunday morning starts at 9 a.m. and a worship service can both happen at the same time and same room. Also [that building] is a Locked Down (all zones) except those visitors for inmates at 9 a.m. until 2 p.m.

Lastly a comment I will make and not dwell on it is, how can ethically a religious advisor be involved in fights for two last Christmases. A thief could also be a liar!

12-23-19 – Monday

I'll try to not be as long this date as I was yesterday.

I woke up early this morning and traditionally put on my glaucoma drops for my eyes, then had my prayer time with God, and then arose and put on my knee high support hose to keep my right leg from swelling so much. That leg is where physicians harvested a vein to install in my heart for my triple by-pass in 2016.

Then the face wash and combing my hair. I heat up my cup of instant coffee and rolled out into the hall to visit with friends while waiting for the truck to deliver breakfast.

So, what is on the agenda for today? We will have mop up in about an hour. Then I may just lay down and take a nap since we do not have the creative writing class this Monday.

Power nap over—power not needed, nothing to do. Think man think, find something constructive to do. Think! Think! OK, I am continuing my work on revising some of my novels. There is more sentence structure to be checked. Proper use of words to be considered, more descriptions of people, places, and things to be added, and possibly even situations to be restructured or even changed. "See you have plenty of work to be done, so mentally and physically get at it!" OK!

I found something to do, but I am lucky to be able write and have the education to compose stories into novels, be they ever so simple, but I am learning from my writing class!

What about that other 90% inmates that have nothing to do except sleep, eat, create problems, join gangs, and just in general use only ½ of 1% of their brain instead of the traditional 10%. They need something to occupy, stimulate, or inspire their whole body, mind, and soul. During my 7½ years here so far I have seen inmates that have found their ability to make items from plastic trash bags, the inside of potato chip bags, design and make every imaginable occasional cards, beautiful hand drawn and colored, thinking of you, thank you, and birthday cards, and virtually anything that can be imagined to create or build. Still we have that 90% of inmates that are left with nothing to do but create confusion.

MDOC needs on staff, paid or volunteers, that can create programs of adequate training of fields of work for inmates to learn so when parole time arrives they are mentally ready to work. I do not mean here these dodos that want a title and a salary and do no work. Certainly it takes money that MDOC does not have but that hurdle can be overcome by a top management that knows how to delegate and manage, not some one that has climbed the ladder by attrition and can comprehend and manage about 20% of his responsibility.

"OK, now smart alec, where does the money come from to get these people?" Start with what we have! MDOC houses medical chronic elderly until they, through age, just dry up and blow away, but at the same time the costs for these people runs from $50,000 annually plus to over $150,000 to $250,000 and other than the shortfall in the state allotted money, MDOC has a cash flow from the federal government from elderly and disabled social security and V.A. benefits ranging from $20,000 to $30,000. $20,000 to $30,000 income vs. $50,000 to $250,000 expenses does not really compute to anything but a massive deficit that can accumulate to $40,000,000 to over $60,000,000 expense factor, according to how many 60 and older are kept housed, clothed, food, security, and modestly kept. You say but those are criminals, but they are in many ways incapacitated to the point—mentally and physically—that they are no longer a danger to anybody.

Another benefit to releasing those geriatric bundles is when they are returned to society the family or nursing homes benefits along with the local economy by spending V.A. and S.S. benefits. The federal government at a cost provides Medicare for health expense and the parolee purchases with his own money supplemental insurance, the S.S. and V.A. benefits are spent locally into the economy. The inmate, family, state of Mississippi, and MDOC all win, some more than others!

These geriatric parolees, by health problems are not able to be violent geriatric criminals, even if they wanted to be.

In closing my diary for today, I must emphasize that I am a dumb ass criminal that only wants to screw, maim, or kill, as listed by MDOC and Mississippi legal standards. We can't figure out things like this, "stay out of big business you criminal, and we will tell you when you have been rehabilitated"—probably never, by management!

That's all folks for today!

12-24-19 – Christmas Eve – Tuesday

Well I did it again. I wrote more yesterday than the day before. Sorry. Some time I just can't find a stopping place.

OK, it's Christmas Eve. Been looking out my window frequently, northwards to see if I see any contrails created by reindeer, but thus far nothing and it's nearing sunset. I really didn't expect to see any signs of Santa because he has too many children to attend to and I suppose a 78 year old is on the bottom of his list, but I will keep an eye out for anything that is quite obese and jolly. I am not going to watch any more for Santa because I have already been given the greatest gift I could ever receive and it comes from God. God gave His Son so that I may have everlasting and eternal life through Jesus Christ.

Good night and thank you God!

12-25-19 – Christmas Day – Wednesday

Christmas 2019 has finally arrived. I am hoping I will be home next Christmas. If I am I am going to cook a dinner that I have not had in 7½ years of confinement in this hell hole of humanity that is propagated by MDOC and because of ignorance backed by the State of Mississippi citizens. I wager if the citizens of Mississippi actually and in reality comprehended the actions of the MDOC management, 99.99999999% would vote to ouster this management and try anybody else. I tend to think the Feds are aware of the massiveness and how deep and widespread the graft, greed, and abuses go that they know that probably a trillion dollars or more may be required in an attempt to correct and repair this problem. It is a known fact that Mississippi has the worst legal system in the United States.

Now, back to my original thoughts, since I temporarily sidetracked myself.

If I am home next Christmas it will truly be an old fashioned Christmas at my house! By that I mean the boys, their spouses, their children, grandchildren, friends, and any other relative or friend that wants to attend the Christmas Day on Friday meal is welcome. Friends will enjoy the Christmas Day (Friday) meal then leave, but the rest (the close family) will enjoy the weekend meals. They will start leaving some time Sunday p.m.

At occasions such as this a food table is always set up ready for a person to stop and get a lite meal or a passer-by that grabs a snack, fill their mouth, and continues on his or her way. By the time the last person leaves, a sea food meal will have been eaten along with a southern fried chicken and a bar-b-que meal, and a requested meal where people request a specific dish is cooked. By the end Sunday night five or six cakes, eight or nine pies and any other requested has been cooked and devoured. That has been my old fashioned Christmas each year before MDOC interrupted it.

I am so anxious to get back to my family gatherings and just let me cook, cook, and cook some more.

12-26-19 – Thursday

Yesterday, even though I am in prison was a great day. Of course it was Christmas, but at the end of the day I called two brothers in Jackson that have become personal friends and visited with them for 20 minutes. They were on their way back from Alabama where they visited their father and other relatives. I wished them a very Merry Christmas and a happy and prosperous New Year 2020.

Then I called my youngest son and wife at Diamond Head, MS near Biloxi. Then I called my other son that is currently living in my house in Tate County. He and his wife are divorced. Also his two nephews (sons of my young son) live with them. They are not married. The nephews are all in their early 20s. Everybody works in that household. I don't permit healthy young people to laze around unemployed. I had to work, their father works, so they will also!

So yesterday was a fantastic day and the ending to the day was even better.

Tiffani Martin

This Christmas

It was just two years ago that I was waking up to my 10-year-old daughter's smiling face. During the Christmas season, I would go in the living room after waking her up and unplug the many Christmas lights she and I so beautifully decorated outside as well as the Christmas tree we put up together. When Christmas Day came, I took lots of pictures, as I captured every facial expression behind the opening of each gift. Afterwards, we went to the country and spent the day with my parents, brothers, nieces, nephews, aunts, uncles, and cousins. Many people across the world usually spend Christmas day putting smiles on their children's' faces and fellowshipping with their loved ones.

This Christmas, just like last year, I'm incarcerated as we have entered the holiday season. The scenery itself is the first thing that's noticeably different from my norm. I now wake up each morning to my 100-plus roommates. Some of them believe, some of them don't, and some of them are some downright Grinches. I'm not able to ride down the streets and see the homes decorated with nativities, lighted wreaths, and blow-up snowmen. My sight is filled with barbed wire fences, gray concrete floors, and beige cinder block walls. Some of the ladies here have attempted to get in the spirit of Christmas by decorating with stockings, reindeer, and Santa pictures that they drew and colored. On Christmas morning, I will build up the confidence to call my daughter to wish her a Merry Christmas and try to hold back the tears as we both wish we were spending it together. As my family gathers together to bless and eat the meal that my mom will carefully put together with love, I'll be sitting on my rack waiting to hear the guard on duty yell, "Going back!" That's the call to go to the mess hall. I'll take my small white salt packets with me to give my dinner flavor and hope that the meal is not cold and that my vegetables are bug-free this time. Later that evening when I'm hungry again, I'll eat a pack of Ramen Noodles to try to fill the emptiness. I'll call home that night one more time just to make sure my daughter made it through the day okay and let her and my parents know that I've done the same. I'll find something on TV and dream and wish aloud with the other ladies about how "Imma do that when I get out," as we often do.

There is a lady somewhere wishing for a diamond tennis bracelet or the latest Apple product. For me, the best gift this year is knowing that someone thought enough about me to send me a Christmas card, and if I'm really lucky it will include pictures. Yes, we are convicts, and the Mississippi Prison System makes sure everyone knows it by tagging it on our backs. But before we were convicts, we were ladies, someone's mother, daughter, sister, aunt, or cousin. We still have love in our hearts and emotions that God created us with. So this Christmas the other inmates and I will love and comfort each other as we go through this holiday season. Merry Christmas.

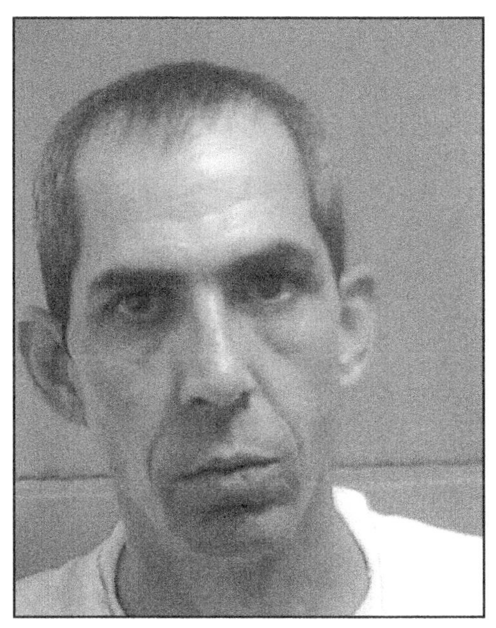

Michael Orrell

Trapped

In retrospect, I began Abstract Art a little over two years ago. I have seen the style of my art evolve, but I also see the need for improvement. I did not even know what abstract meant. The Oxford Dictionary defines abstract as follows: "(of art) achieving its effects by shapes and colors rather than by realism." Some of my art is definitely not realism, according to a few of the pieces that I have created, but other pieces do deal with realism. The Merriam-Webster Dictionary describes this form of art in two words: abstract expressionism. Abstract expressionism was defined by Merriam-Webster as follows: "art that expresses the artists' attitudes and emotions through abstract forms."

I had never heard of Abstract Art or Abstract Expressionism in my entire life until the age of 44. I did not know that Abstract Art began in the 1900s. The Merriam-Webster Dictionary reveals that a man with abstract artistic abilities is given a title: abstract expressionist. I enjoy Merriam-Webster's definition of abstract better than the Oxford Dictionary's definition. Abstract is the style of art that I am passionate about in this part of my life. I love the structure and chaos in abstract art. At times, I will have complete chaos in some pieces because it is easier and more relaxing. But there are other times when I will not take the easy route, and I allow the piece to become more structured. Other times, I have a balance of both structure and chaos. I am also the first artist to bring abstract art to Parchman. Overall, I have a very intrigued audience because my style is different. I am different.

The art pieces entitled "Trapped" and "Cross of Confusion" are highly demonized by a majority of the Christian audience, few of whom understood the meaning of my gift. I appreciate those that appreciate my creations, but I will not allow critical opinions to keep me from being an abstract expressionist. My art has a name: C.A.T.A. Vision (Contemporary Abstract Tribal Art) Vision. As for those that demonize my art, whether religious or secular, they are entitled to their opinion. Opinions are like butt holes: everybody has one. Their opinions are like water on a duck's back.

Before creating the "Trapped" piece, I had no earthly idea what the title would be, nor did I know what the piece would actually become until the flow was over. After the last Creative Writing Class for the holidays, I completed "Trapped" eight days later. I was satisfied with the completion of it, but I was also dissatisfied because I did not understand what it was saying. I put it under my mat where it sat for a couple of days. I began to observe it closely, and the piece began to speak to me by saying, "Michael, you are trapped in your melancholy (sadness and depression), and your anger (madness and aggression)." I have heard, "Art imitates life." That statement is a true one. What I saw and heard about this piece revealed something that has always played a role in my life: anger and depression.

I know the viciousness of sexual abuse and cruel physical abuse. I was filled with so much anger that my Creator deserted me to such dark circumstances, but I no longer considered myself the victim. I became angry and sad about my becoming a victimizer. How could I do such horrible things to others as was done to me? I have come to hate myself for what I did to the innocent. My twisted sexual immorality had me angry with myself, and the sadness of what I did was overwhelming. I will never justify my actions by the things done to me for the things I have done to others. I was the victim that became a victimizer who has become the victor. The tragedy and trauma in my life has turned to triumph. Finally, I have moved on into another chapter in my life by forgiving those that harmed me, by asking those that I harmed to forgive me, and finally by forgiving myself. Forgiveness is for you and not them. If I choose not to forgive, then I will only become a tormented person. No more will I be a man of torment.

Look at the piece entitled "Trapped." Notice the four suns in each corner. Two suns are angry, and the other two are sad. Notice how the horns, razors, spikes, and teeth face inwardly. They are not facing outwardly as if protecting them. These suns are trapped. I was trapped in my madness and sadness, which became my reason for my insanity.

Notice how the sad suns are the color of blue. I did not intentionally color them blue. Think about how people describe sadness as feeling blue. The horns, razors, spikes, and the sharp teeth represent the pain of these cutting, piercing, slicing, and puncturing objects. This is how it feels when a person is trapped in anger and depression.

Now look at the bottom at the three aliens. Because of my angry attitude, no one wanted to befriend me, and so I felt as if I did not belong: like an alien. The depression caused me to alienate myself from the few people that would speak to me.

Observe the center piece which consists of the greatest sun, which is a malicious and murderous one. It is trapped in two arrows: one pointing Eastward and on pointing Westward. It is symbolic of how unending my anger was. It had turned me into a homicidal and suicidal maniac, and people came to fear me and did not want to be near me. Notice the background which is black and symbolic of the darkness.

The beauty of this piece lies only in the realization that the darkness of anger and depression is no longer the god of my life. On January 16, 2016, a friend and fellow prisoner died right before my eyes, and his death hit me hard. Things happen to us or around us for a purpose. Whether we see it or not, that is left up to us, but it would be wise to see it as something that the Creator is trying to tell us. Allen (A.D.) died, and it made me realize that we have no promise of tomorrow. I have reconciled my differences with a lot of people because I don't want to live my life in regret any longer. It steals joy.

William McCain

Ramblings from a Tired and Broken Lifer

I say that I don't write poems, cause frankly I hate Poetry.

But now I sit and write: problem is, I don't have a damn clue what I might say.

As I sit here on a bunk made of metal in a building not made of much more, just like an old warehouse, not much more than a big tin box.

This is where they send you when things go wrong and you break the law, not that you broke the law on purpose, but now you're no longer fit to be a member of the public.

One very bad action, a very bad mistake, never been in trouble with the law before in your life, and that's exactly what they give you: a life sentence in prison. Forget the key. They won't need that anymore. They don't ever expect to let you leave.

Cram you like an overstocked chicken house in a big tin building sitting in wide open land and no kind of shade from the sweltering heat of the Mississippi Delta.

Locked down over every little thing, no canteen, no visits. Then they turn off the phone: not being allowed to call home to talk to Mama. That's just plain wrong. To punish us inmates for no good reason is bad enough, but why should our families have to suffer and be denied visits with their loved ones? You try so very hard not to get in any trouble by breaking any rules, but what's the point when you can be punished and not had to do anything wrong.

I try to be good and keep my living area clean, and I'll be damned if I don't get an R.V.R. while in my rack asleep.

Life in prison, there can't be much worse; I wish I could turn time in reverse.

If I had a time machine, I'd go back in time to when I was 16. To when life was easy and times were fun. Just to be a kid again playing in the sun. No boundaries and no fences, steel bars or locked doors.

Life was so much easier when I was just a young boy, riding bikes all over the neighborhood or pushing Tonka trucks around in the dirt. Mom was happy as long as I didn't get hurt.

I often sit and wonder where I went wrong, and I'm pretty sure it was the day I left home. My life from that point went badly off course, and I caught a ride on a fast train straight to destruction.

Wind and rain may cause us a little pain. Life in this jungle will surely make me go insane.

If my life were a movie, it would be called Nightmare on My Street.

Friday the 13th or Nightmare on Elm Street: if it were Jason verses Freddie, Jason would probably get a beat down.

Michael Myer's Jason, or Freddie Krueger? I'd hang out with Freddie because no one could be cooler. He might as well be called the dream ruler. He finds you in your dreams and kills you in your sleep. I'd rather have him on my side than grabbing at my feet.

If I were a bird, I'd be an eagle, soaring high above the clouds, dropping low to piss on a crowd.

Eyes so strong and talons so sharp, he can zoom in on a rat from 3,000 feet, then use his talons to tear apart the meat.

Grass on the ground, stars in the sky, if I were a bat, far away is where I'd fly.

If I could leave prison, I'd never come back. I've spent enough nights on this hard ass rack.

Now if you can't make sense out of all this chatter, it's just to kill time and it doesn't even matter.

Tara R. Lyle

The First 30 Days

This was only the second time I had been in the back of a patrol car. The very first time was the day of my arrest.

This day I had left the county jail and was on my way to prison for killing my husband. It had only been a few days since my trial. At this point, I'm not sure what I was feeling. I kept replaying images of my oldest daughter falling out in court upon hearing my guilty verdict. I couldn't even comfort her or tell her that we all would eventually be okay. I'm sure my youngest daughter was feeling scared and uncertain because once again her life had been forever changed.

I was trying to imagine what prison would be like as I rode in the back of the cruiser. My only sources were two of the ladies I'd been housed with at the county jail. That information passed on was their own personal experiences. I felt and knew somehow my experience would be totally different … because I had a life sentence with a murder charge.

Sure enough, I wouldn't follow the course of the conventional prisoner (or the majority of female offenders). I learned early on as I was being processed that I would have to spend up to two years in solitary confinement, which was housed in the maximum security unit. That news alone sent a wave of tears flowing down my face. I thought if they only knew that I wasn't a violent person, even though I committed a violent act—they wouldn't have to send me to Solitary Confinement, where I would be in a cell by myself 23 hours a day with one hour to go outside.

After I was finished being processed, I was loaded on a van so that I could be taken to MSU (the maximum-security unit). All I had in tow was my Bible that I certainly clung to and the clothing the State had issued me. I felt as though I was in a foreign and desolate land.

How would I let my family know where I was now located? Would I be able to receive mail? Would I even survive this solitary confinement? "Ma'am, why are you crying?" asked the security guard who drove me to MSU. I was too distraught to answer, so I just hung my head and allowed my tears to continue to fall. Her last words to me were, "You will make it."

The cell door was finally opened for me to go in. The only thing in the cell was a sink and commode. There was not even a bunk present. The guard eventually brought me a flattened single-size mattress to sleep on. I remember positioning the mattress against the wall and sitting on the mattress with my back against the wall, wondering how I would be able to make it through this. My heart ached for all the people I'd hurt and disappointed. My heart ached that I couldn't be present to comfort my two daughters. My heart ached that I'd allowed myself to stay in a marriage that I should have ended a long time ago. My heart ached that I had shot and killed a man I truly loved. My heart ached that I was now a ward of the State. When I did finally fall asleep, I had my Bible clutched in my arms. Hugging my Bible did provide a sense of comfort as I tried to still my mind.

For the days that followed, I began the slow process of adjustment. At certain times, I was able to start speaking with some of the other inmates on my cell block. It was during the times that the guards would open our slots that were used to pass our trays through. I began to look forward to the times that our slots were opened because it provided a gateway to my immediate community, although we all were behind closed doors.

My routine at night was going to sleep hugging my Bible. It had not only become my source of inspiration but also my security blanket as well.

By the end of my first month of incarceration, my nightly routine came to a screeching halt after a conversation with one of my sisters. I'd shared with her how I never missed sleeping with my Bible at night. I didn't anticipate her next response, but it was a sobering one. She told me I needed to stop sleeping with my Bible at night because I was sleeping with it out of fear. I couldn't argue with her statement, and I told her from then on, I wouldn't sleep with my Bible anymore; and I didn't.

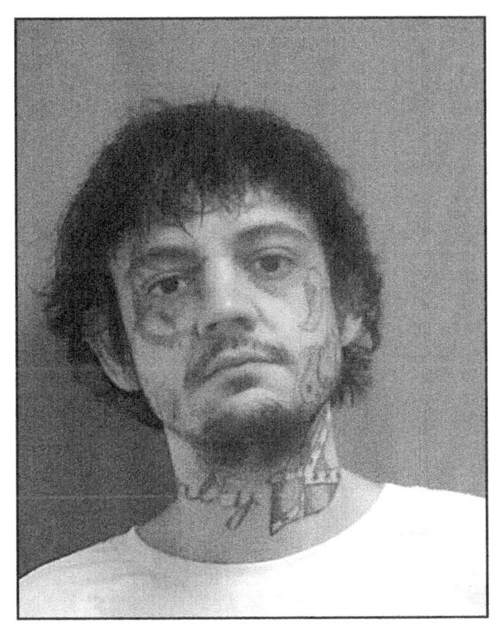

Tyler Graham

My Apology

I would like to apologize to the world. I feel I need to apologize after reflecting on myself and my actions thus far in life. I will start by apologizing to my family. I'm not the man that I am "supposed" to be for you guys. I am a selfish person. I have done and still do things to make you guys push me away. Even knowing how much I hurt you guys, I still choose to do the things that make me happy with absolutely no thought of how it will affect the ones around me. You have done so much for me. I know you don't understand because most times I don't understand myself or my actions. Now I would like or feel the need to apologize to the ones that live around me at this very moment and to those who have lived around me during my incarceration. I honestly do my best to get along with everyone, to be a "convict," a "team-player," but sometimes my own thoughts, things I hear or think I hear, the way I feel, make me do things that I know aren't normal or things that even push fellow convicts away. I realize my actions are not "normal." I sometimes wonder what is normal? Who gets to set these standards everyone is held to and examined against? Obviously not me, or anyone like me. So I apologize to family and fellow convicts. Now, one last person I would like to apologize to is myself. I am the one I hurt the most. I am a selfish, drug addicted, lying, manipulating bastard: I am a crap of a person. Most call it being a product of my environment, but there is no viable excuse for the way I am and it is going to catch up with me. It has been catching up with me for years and will probably be the death of me. I pray every day for someone, anyone, God, family, whoever or whatever, to set me straight, to change my ways, to make me care a little bit more about everything that matters and leave alone the things that hurt everyone involved. So this is my apology to the world. I am sorry for being me.

God forbid you all let me know my shortcomings, downfalls, screw ups, and fuck ups every day. Thanks guys. Thanks for caring! Just what I needed to start the day. So I will do my best to live up to the moral standards you've set, but fair warning: don't hold your breath.

Linda Ross

From Misdiagnosed to Misunderstood

All my life I've been called stupid, dumb, retarded, or told that I was odd, strange, and even weird. I might have even looked the part. I even acted a little goofy to some, shy to others, and was always afraid of my own shadow in school. This was not an act. My actions were partly due to living in a broken home. This was my only way of life and the only home I'd known. From as long as I could remember, my home life was violent. A peaceful home was being molested in one way or another. I didn't start talking until I was four years of age. My primary means of communication was by pointing with my fingers and uttering the one word: "That." I was kept from attending school almost thirty percent of each school year. I would later be sent to a summer school to help with my apparent learning disability. Summer school didn't help at all to bring my failing grades up for the coming year. I just couldn't concentrate on my work in the classroom. I acquired a speech problem, and the other kids began to torment me because of it. At my birth, the doctor had difficulty getting me to breathe. My mother always said that this was the reason behind my slowness and limited conversations with others. I also had a chronic bronchitis asthma condition. Regardless, it never affected my athletic ability to play sports or childhood games with my sister. It was when I got hot, tired, hit hard in my chest or back, then I would suffer from an asthma attack. If I became scared or caught a cold, another attack would be there as well. Most of my childhood, I wore "hand-me-downs" from the Salvation Army, where my mom shopped. I also probably had a smell of overnight urine, as I wet the bed until I was nine. My smelly clothes were probably another reason for other kids to pick on me. I was taken out of a normal public school for almost a year to be seen by a children's mental health specialist. I was diagnosed by this doctor as mildly retarded, and low in adaptive "functionings." By the time I was sent back to school, I had turned five. Instead of riding the "big yellow bus" with my oldest sister again, I was placed on the "short yellow bus" in another school. The kids there did much of nothing all day. They slept or gazed out the window alongside me. I would cry about almost anything. If you yelled, laughed, or touched me, I would cry as well. I cried so much that even my navel was pushed out twice its normal size. I just couldn't seem to learn simple fundamentals of education or even gain common sense for my age group. I didn't understand the things I read. I could spell worth nothing and couldn't work math problems that even second graders could do until I reached the age of twelve. These difficulties helped me to develop a defensive temper. I started fighting the bullies back! The older I got, the more rebellious I became towards authority and those who imposed it. I had a nervous complex which had started at home. I had a hard time staying in my chair at school or anywhere for that matter. It seemed I was always worried about getting back home, in fear my mother would be killed by my stepfather.

It was in my era that violence was everywhere in the streets and the community. The Black Panther movement prompted even more racially motivated assassinations. The Vietnam War was in full swing. There were few jobs, low wages, lots of hard work, small pay for black people. This was always the topic of discussion in my house.

At the age of nineteen, I was once again taken to yet another psychologist for more evaluations. This doctor added more symptoms to an already misdiagnosed mental health file. It contained in my file that I was hearing voices, and had a case of psychosis. Once I started to work towards getting some form of education, my self-esteem was so low it almost seemed impossible to dream of achieving something as grand as my GED. I would like to say to all children born with Down syndrome, bullied for being different, who stuttered or had other disabilities, to never accept what they say, never. Do not ever let people tell you that retards can't accomplish a goal. Your dreams matter! Getting my GED was one more awesome miracle that God performed through me. I'm reminded of a story my teacher, Ms. House, once told me. It was about an eighty-two year old rich man she had tutored part-time. He had told her that he had accomplished everything in life but a college degree. He later got his degree but had a low score, and so did I. Ms. House said that it doesn't matter if you finished at the bottom or on the honor roll. What was important was that you didn't stop: what you finish is what you earned and what you are worth.

Sabrina Williams

What's on Your Mind?

I have a lot on my mind that keeps me puzzled at all times. I think about what I'm going to do when I get home. My seven children are always and constantly on my mind, and I think about going back to school to get a higher education. I plan on opening my own business and making a future for my kids.

I keep God on my mind and how he has blessed me to be able to see another day. He has been a blessing and a tremendous part of my life. I give him all the glory and praise for keeping me and protecting me. Giving God the highest praise even in the midst of trouble and trials and tribulations.

I think about my girlfriend and how she got busted down and went to Red & White and then to Max. I constantly keep on my mind that I need to keep a leveled head and remain calm, cool, and collected. I sometimes feel as though I need peace-of-mind and some time, because I know me and I know how I am and how I get at times. So, I take deep breaths to keep from having an anxiety attack and from getting upset enough to where I am angry and lashing out at people. I try to keep my anger and temper under control as much as I possibly can. These are the things that are on my mind.

JOURNAL

1-30-18 I enjoyed class today, and I realized my worth and my potential. I wrote home to my sister and my dad to see how they were doing. I wrote my friend to let her know how I was doing and how I was keeping myself sane. I feel lost at times and sometimes I feel like I need some time to myself away from others.

1-31-18 I woke up today with tears in my eyes after crying last night because my girlfriend is in Red & White and in Max. I woke up to a bunch of drama and problems. I got on my knees and prayed to God to take away all problems and to help me make it through the day. I feel he wakes me up for a reason every day, and I thank Him every day for what he does in my life.

2-1-18 I woke up to the good grace of God, for He is the reason I am living and breathing. I prayed for my kids and my family and their safety. I even prayed that I will have a good and blessed day today.

2-2-18 Pocket-Size Prayer: Father, You are good. I need help; heal me and forgive me. They need help. Thank you.

2-3-18 Prayer: We give our hearts to you, Lord. Please teach us to be humble. We give our feet to you, Lord. Please help us not to stumble. Our eyes belong to you, Lord, to see your Holy Way. Help us to look straight ahead and seek you every day. With our ears let us hear you, Lord, every time you call. We give ourselves to you, Lord. We will obey your Law. We give our hands to you, Lord. We lift them up in praise. We will worship you, Lord, all our blessed days. Our mouth we give to you, Lord. We shout with victory. We belong to you, Lord. Now we are living free.

AMEN!

2-4-18 We had a blast at the yard party yesterday! We had popcorn, hot dogs, and Gatorade, along with the puppies. We got to see people we haven't seen since we moved to the yard from Quick Bed. It was like a big family reunion with no problems, none whatsoever.

2-5-18 Psalm 91

2-6-18 Psalm 41

2-7-18 I went on a fast today so that I can find out who I really am in my own eyes and God's eyes. I meditated and distanced myself from others.

2-8-18 to 2-14-18 Fasting

2-15-18 to 2-19-18 Sick

Edward Kennedy Carroll

Trauma Experienced as a Child

My childhood trauma began at the age of sixteen years old. In the City of New Orleans, downtown. Coming up was hard, yet still my parents manage to support my every need as a child. Like every other neighborhood, there were drug dealers at every corner you turned. But that's not what brought trauma into my life at all. It was the loss of my beloved father. His name was Charles Edward Kennedy. My dad worked his whole life making sure the family had everything we needed. Growing up under my father and mother's household with my brother and sister, Frederick and Charlene, it was very hard because my father was very hard on us as children. We didn't have too many friends. Mostly it was always family. And he used to tell me all the time, "Son, go to school so one day you can find yourself a good paying job." Advice which I always took heed to.

In the year 1997, summer time it was.... I wanted to hang out with some of my school mates around the corner from where I lived. So then, I went and asked my father can I join a few of my buddies from my school, and my dad replied, "NO, I don't want you hanging with them Hoodlums!" So, I went to my room and said to myself, "Man you can't do nothing. It makes me sick!" So, then I snuck out the back door of my house and jumped a few gates to hang out with my buddies around the corner.

Now at this time, my dad noticed that I was missing and checked everywhere in the house and couldn't find me anywhere. So he left my mother at the house and told her, "I'll be right back!" And he took out on foot to find me and walked the neighborhood, and that's when he found me smoking a blunt of weed. And my daddy found me around the corner, and he began to whip me in front of my friends all the way back home. I felt so bad. Then around the year of 1998, Easter Sunday, my father passed away due to a heart attack. My whole world flipped because I knew the loss of him would hurt the family dearly. Two kids who always had their father in their life, and then he was gone within a blink of an eye. Boy, did I cry: I never knew I'd miss his presence that badly. And my mom telling me everything is gonna be all right was not good enough. My life began breaking bad.... The trauma I experienced due to the loss of my dad made me turn to them streets, guns, drugs, and women, being out all night, and eventually I stopped caring about a lot of things. My life became so bad to the point that all I cared about was the streets. I was so far gone with a mind that had zero understanding for nothing and no one, and my life's been hell ever since.

Having someone I cared about so much despite the experience I had with that person played a big part in my life, and the loss of my dad turned out completely bad. But at the same time you live and learn, and that's just the way life is for every woman, man, and child. Life is what you make of it, good or bad, but trauma plays some type of part in the things you experience in life that were bad. But in my situation, the loss of someone I loved and cared about made me go astray, and I wish that person was still on the face of this earth. Maybe things would be different in my life. But as I continue to express this trauma that I've experienced from my childhood unto adulthood, it makes me feel bad because this was not the path my parents set for me coming up. Now this experience of trauma, due to the loss of a loved one and the choices I've made has pushed me to a place I never want to be again ever in life. And that place is jail, lockdown, away from my family. But that's a price you pay due to your own actions in life. Not every situation is the same, but as you become one with yourself, you will see things for what they are, and not what you make of it. So now I see it the truth of things as being a man. But when you lost someone at a young age, you will feel lost with no sense of direction, and that can happen to anybody. So it's something common dealing with boys becoming a man, but from the beginning to the end, it's all real life as I tell this story about my childhood trauma as a child. And every man, woman, and child all make mistakes and are held accountable for their own actions. The experience of the pain I felt still affects me to this very day, and I don't think I'll ever be over it.

Growing Up on Dirt

Comin' up in poverty, where you got to get out the dirt, wearing off-brand shoes, and getting food stamps to get by month to month. It was my lil' brother Fred and my lil sister Charlene, and my mom and dad. The house was very over crowded, forcing us to go outside. The house was a three-bed room with no A\C in the summertime. We had to use box fans, one in each room, which didn't do very much. My father only worked one job to support three kids. He could be lot on a man. He would always find a way to make sure he got us what we needed. It was just his way of doing things. Old fashioned. And I would always say things, asking why we didn't have cable or why we didn't have nice shoes. Why we didn't have a nice house. I always wondered about these kinds of things coming up as and child. So, as I got older, I began to understand the ways of the world and why things were the way they were in those days. Everybody poor, living month after month on food stamps or getting some type of help from the Government or some kind of low-budget job. Trying to get by. But with the loss of my father, it all hit me at once, cause then I realized we were really Poor.

So now can you picture a single black woman raising three kids and living on food stamps trying to pay the bills, lights, water, and gas, plus the rent, my mother having to pay all things and making sure the kids are good at the same time. And my sister and brother and me went from wearing nothing to All Stars to Putting on XJ900s, to eating butter bread 3X's a day because all the food would be gone before the month was over with. Yet, still we managed to make it somehow. As the years went and came, times became even harder for us. I would like to call it the Hard Knock Life, because it was more like the more I saw, the worse I started wanting the things I saw my friends have, but my mom was unable to provide them for me. So I turned to the streets selling drugs, weed, crack cocaine, and doing all the wrong things to get money. I knew the things I was doing were wrong, but it was a fast lifestyle, and I got used to it real fast. I was doing a good job at helping my mother with the bills, putting food on the table, dressing real nice, making that cash. But you know how the story goes: all good things must come to an end when you're not living the right way and, being young minded, at the same time thinking I'm doing the right things. So, at the end of all this story, I was made a bad person because I wanted money and wanted to live good since it was so hard for me and the rest of my family. Coming up was bad and hard in the city of New Orleans, a lot of good times and hard times. But in my neighborhood, you make a way when it's no way out, and that's the way it's gonna be.

So can you picture thousands of families that are going through these times with nothing to eat, no lights, water, or gas, unable to pay the rent, just straight out poor. It's something that will stick with you over the years. Forced to turn to the streets because life wasn't what you wanted it to be. But sometimes you got to make the best of it, no matter how hard times may be, and I call it Life. Cause everybody's not going to have it all in life and that's just the way it is. Now days us young people want and are used to the finest things in life, and I'm one of them people—young money, fast cars, fast everything. . . is what they want, and they pretty much will do anything to make it that way. I know you expect me to sit here on my bed and write this to make you feel good about everything, but I'm not one of those kind of people: I can't sit here and lie to you people. The streets raised me and made me. Cause I always wanted the best things in life, even as a kid, and I'll tell anybody reaching for the stars and beyond that you better watch what you reach for! That's just being real. And I want to tell my mom I know I messed up and I'm sorry for telling you I went to school, when I'd been on the corner all day getting money. Forgive me. I wanted to have the best things in life and they don't come free. You got to pay hard and work hard to make things better for yourself. No matter what the situation may be or how much I try to explain it, you people will not understand it. We was poor, way down in the dirt, and that ain't nothing easy to come out of.

Jennifer Thomas

Wicked Blessed

My life has been incredibly disastrous and full of infinite failure wrapped in total Chaos. A few years ago, I would've said that I have orchestrated and set myself up for my own demise. With having failed my children, my mother, my whole family, myself, and this chance I had at life. Today I say, "The upside in setbacks…fuels new dreams." This is only the beginning of the rest of my life. I have truly been blessed for this lesson learned. This, I shall not take for granted.

I've been incarcerated for four years. I'm a mother of five beautiful children. I have three daughters, and my youngest two are boys. I became a mother at the age of sixteen. I grew up way too fast, just not in the responsible and mature kind of way. I've made a lot of wrong decisions and bad choices. When you're young, sometimes you just have to learn from your own mistakes. I can say, though, I do not regret my life's actions for they are what has brought me to this point of recognition in my life. It's a wise one who learns from her mistakes.

A lot of the women locked up in here with me say that they feel as if their lives have been taken from the time that they were incarcerated. Even the majority of these people still come right back. You hear stories, thousands of different stories by thousands of different people. Seems as though most feel like prison has robbed them of their lives, made them lose their children, homes, friends, etc. Most have no understanding that we are the ones at fault. We made the wrong choices that consequently landed us here in prison.

On the day that I got sentenced, when I got back in my cell to lie down for the night, I prayed. I had the most in-depth conversation that I have ever had in my entire life with God. I, of course, asked Him for His help. Even though our relationship hasn't been too good, I bowed my head and asked only for a few things. I did not ask to come home or ask why this happened to me. I simply asked him to come into my heart and fill me with the peace and contentment that I need to not stress and worry about the things that I cannot change while I do my time and overcome any trials and tribulations. I just needed the strength. Since that very night my heart has had almost like a shield of armor over it and will not allow me to worry. Now, I am only to become stronger.

The lessons that I have learned are just amazing. I have found patience, wisdom, knowledge, and understanding. When you have everything that you love and care about taken from you, the world that you were so used to changes completely. That really does something to a person. It really did something to me.

I carry the title of a mother, a sister, a daughter, an aunt, and a wife. Now coming to this realization, have I ever really been any of these things that I claim I truly cherish? Have I ever actually fit the part? Clearly, I now see that I was flying through life not even knowing its true meaning.

I'm very thankful that I have received a second chance at life. A chance to improve and to consider every little thing and not miss any little details. Promising not to take another day for granted. You never know what tomorrow will bring. Or if God will bring a tomorrow. I know that I cannot make up for lost time, but I can make sure that I don't have to lose any more. Life is way too short. Some things you don't even have time for when all you do have is time.

Prison has saved my family and my life. Because prison has saved me. It gave me the time that I couldn't find to open my mind, body, and soul. Without it, I would have hurt a lot of people. Never even realizing it, or better yet, never even taking the time to care. With that being said, prison to me has been one of my greatest blessings. A true blessing in disguise.

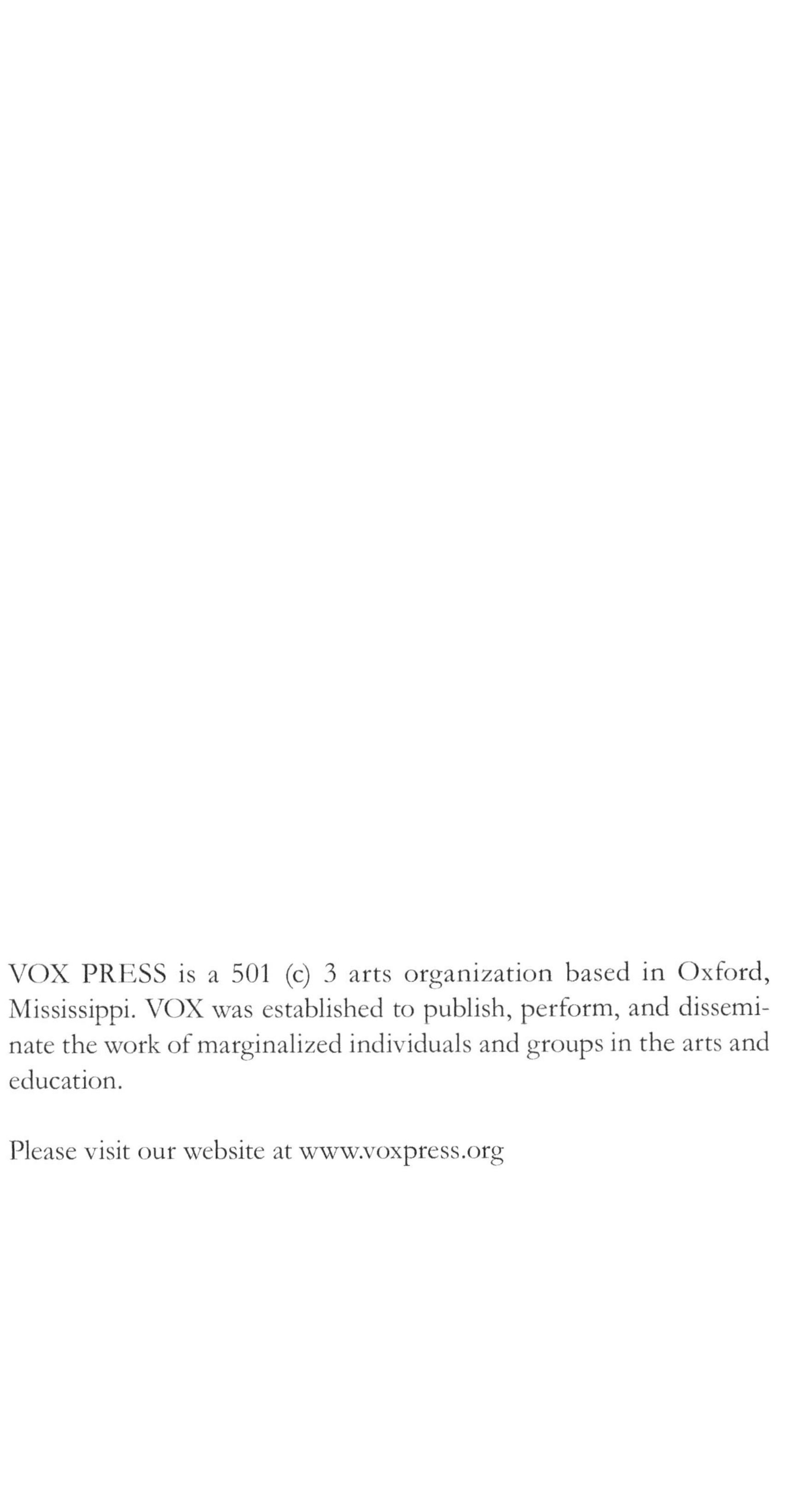

VOX PRESS is a 501 (c) 3 arts organization based in Oxford, Mississippi. VOX was established to publish, perform, and disseminate the work of marginalized individuals and groups in the arts and education.

Please visit our website at www.voxpress.org

Made in the USA
Monee, IL
27 July 2021

74373827R00144